TALES FROM A RURAL ROUTE

HENRY COUNTY HIGH SCHOOL: VOLUME II

Edited by

KARIN M. ACREE

ISBN: 978-1-937979-64-5

Twin Sisters Press
Goshen, Kentucky 40026
www.twinsisterspress.com

INTRODUCTION

I met the Henry County High School students for the first time several years ago at the Kentucky Book Fair. It was the Friday before the full book fair, dedicated to children and librarians. I decided to attend on Friday, hoping my books may be of interest to the "adults" tagging along with the kids.

The Henry County students stood out for both their love of books and their willingness to engage me in witty banter—something I hold in high regard.

I met Rachel Burgin, the school's library media specialist and all around fabulous person, and offered to come talk to the students about writing. Not long after, she extended an invitation to me. I suggested we hold a short story contest and with the help of the English teachers, *Tales From a Rural Route: Henry County High School* was born in 2017.

The writing program was so successful we decided to do it again the next school year, leading to the book you are now reading, *Tales From a Rural Route: Henry County High School Volume II*.

I am constantly amazed at the talent and effort the students put forth in their writing and I could not be more proud of their success.

I look forward to many more years of partnering with the faculty, staff and students of Henry County High School and watching the students grow as writers.

Tony Acree
    Publisher
    Twin Sisters Press

ANOTHER WORLD

By Gracie Golden

Vada rolled her eyes. "Would you all just be quiet? Goodness gracious," she snapped. Her family was going on vacation and twenty minutes into the three hour drive, Vada was already annoyed by her three siblings. They were telling jokes too corny for a scarecrow and snorting like pigs. Luckily, earbuds and smartphones with music existed. Soon enough, Vada drifted off to her favorite K-Pop band.

She fell asleep quickly and immediately began dreaming. It was a dream she had frequently ever since she was young, though it varied sometimes. It has been more frequent lately. In her dream, she woke up and jumped out of a big bed surrounded by fluffy down blankets. She walked out of her room and into a hallway. It's a really big hallway, like one you would find in a castle. There are stain glass windows letting a soft glow into the hallway; a peaceful scene. She walked to the windows and glanced out a plain one where she sees a beautiful sea glistening beneath her. The dream gives her a sense of belonging.

But the chaos in the courtyard turned her stomach. Men dressed in red uniforms and others in navy blue are fighting mercilessly and ferociously. There are bodies scattered all around the grass. There are footsteps coming from the hallway on her left. Two soldiers in red were running right at her. She hiked up the skirt of her nightgown and took off to her right. She sprinted as fast as she could, but the soldiers were, well, soldiers. Vada could hear a loud scrape as the soldiers drew their swords. She panicked. A hand grabbed her arm and pulled her roughly into a room. It was the main quarters of the highest royal living in the castle. The person who pulled her in was wearing navy blue; he was a good guy. He didn't say anything only extended his hand. A black hole appeared, then turned gold, then a bright red. The door suddenly burst open. Some invisible force pushed Vada forward into a red hole. She was falling through walls of red. Her arms were flailing. She was screaming.

CRASH! Vada slammed hard against the back of the seat in front of her, instantly waking from her dream. But what she woke up to was a nightmare. Water was filling the cab of the car. The summer sunlight was ascending over the surface of the river their car had fallen into. Vada frantically unbuckled, but didn't know what to do next.

"Roll down the windows!" her dad shouted to them through. Vada's eleven year old sister, Jenna, was crying in the backseat, and her nine year old brother, Chase, was whimpering.

"What?!" Vada's seventeen year old brother, Kyle, shrieked.

"Roll them down and get out!" their dad shouted. They began cranking the levers of their old car to open the windows. Water poured in. Vada forgot to take a big breath and was instantly assaulted by the water. The window was only three-quarters down but she couldn't breathe. Vada, who was thin and lanky, easily slipped through the open window, abandoning the car. She propelled herself up, up, up.

The surface of the water broke and Vada took the biggest breath she could. She sputtered and coughed up water as her mom and Chase came up, doing the same. A second later, her dad, Kyle, and Jenna popped up. Jenna wasn't crying and Chase wasn't whimpering. They were treading water in shocked silence. Vada looked to her parents. They were staring around them, baffled. In that moment, Vada realized how cold and dark it was. And was that snow falling from the sky?

"Everyone swim to the shore. It's dark, I know, but just swim towards that big mass over there," her dad commanded. He pointed in the distance. Vada could barely make it out, but there indeed was land.

"But, Daddy! What about the car?" Chase asked, breaking his silence.

"There's not really anything we can do for it right now, is there?" their dad snapped.

"Tyler!" their mom cried.

He ignored her and began swimming, and the rest of the family had no choice but to follow.

What seemed like forever passed. Vada's feet finally scraped sand, and a minute later she was crawling onto the snow covered beach. Everyone was coughing and chattering. Vada was shaking violently, though she couldn't tell if it was more from exhaustion or unexplainable cold. *What was going on anyway?* When she fell asleep, it was a sunny summer's day, and when she popped out of the water a minute after the crash, it was a snowy winter's night. It would all be too overwhelming if that sense of belonging she had in her dreams wasn't disrupting her situation.

"We need a fire," their dad announced, shakily standing up.

"And shelter. Let's get out of the open," their mom said. It took her a moment to stand because soreness was quickly setting in, but when she did she helped all her kids stand up. They walked into the forest a little ways away from the shore. Then they hiked. They hiked until they found a clearing surrounded by trees with thick canopies.

"This will work," their dad said, setting down Chase. He had been shivering so much earlier that he could barely walk. Vada gratefully sat on the ground. Jenna crawled into her lap, shaking like a leaf. The kids watched as their parents huddled together and whispered frantically. Vada caught words like fire, alone, hurt, and killed. Her stomach turned to lead. Killed? Who was getting killed?

"Vada, what's happening?" Jenna asked in a whisper. She looked into Vada's eyes. Jenna's usually slightly tanned, freckled face was sheet white and her lips were turning blue. Somehow, it even looked like her blonde hair had dulled. In fact, each of her family members looked like this. Vada wondered if she had turned blue, considering she had dark complected skin.

"How is she supposed to know?" Kyle snapped. He hugged Chase closer to him. Jenna's forehead wrinkled and the corners of her mouth turned down.

Vada knew what was coming next. "Jenna, no, no, no. Don't cry! It's fine. We-we'll figure it out. Don't worry," she said quickly. Jenna nodded and gulped down her tears.

"Fine," their mom burst out in a whisper. They looked up to see their parents making their way back to them.

"Dad, what's going on?" Kyle asked bluntly. Their dad's

stern face softened a bit. He looked at their mom, who nodded, then back at them.

"Guys, we're in a serious situation right now. We don't know what that situation actually is at the moment, but it's a scary one, I know. But you better listen to me right now. Mom and I are going to go look for some dry firewood. It might take a while. Try to stay warm as best you can, but don't make much noise. If you hear something suspicious or think you are in danger, run. Don't worry about mom or I. Just take care of yourselves. Got it?" their dad said. No one made a sound. "Got it?" he asked more forcefully. Vada and Kyle slowly nodded. "Good. Keep each other safe now."

The kids got a kiss and hug from each of their parents. The two adults then trotted quietly across the clearing and disappeared into the dark forest. The four kids sat in silence for the longest time. Vada never imagined something would ever keep her younger siblings from chattering away or asking questions. She found their "silencer." Vada began French braiding Jenna's hair out of boredom. She always French-braided her little sister's hair. She couldn't do it to hers. It was always too poofy to put in a ponytail, let alone a braid.

The wind picked up suddenly.

"Kyle," Chase whispered.

"What?" Kyle asked gruffly.

"What was that noise?"

"What are you talking about?"

"That...that noise!"

"The wind?"

"No! It's different!"

"I can't hear anything."

Vada tuned out her brothers and listened. The wind was blowing, yes. But...wait. What was that? She squinted her eyes;

she did this to hear better. It usually worked. Luckily it worked now. There. In the distance. Rustling leaves, like the wind, but sharper and louder. Crashes of bushes. Leaves and snow crunching. Someone out there was running. Vada's heart jolted.

"I hear it. Guys, I hear what Chase is talking about. We need to go," Vada said in a commanding tone.

"Oh, shove it. You're just a paranoid little girl. Keep it up and you'll make Jenna cry," Kyle spat. He shoved Chase off his lap.

"Kyle, I am not kidding. We need to go. There's someone running out there."

"Just be quiet." Kyle rolled his eyes.

Vada groaned. The running sounds were growing louder. "You heard what Dad said. If there's something suspicious, we need to run. Me and Chase hear it. We need to get out of here!"

"I'm not suspicious. You are. Now sit," Kyle growled. He looked up at Vada, who was towering over him. She's always been incredibly tall, and he had just caught up to her a month ago.

"No Kyle, we need to—"

"RUN!" their mom screeched from somewhere. It echoed around them, bouncing off the canopies.

All of their eyes widened. Kyle was up in a flash. The kids tore through the forest with no regard for stealth. Their muscles were cold, tight, and sore, but their adrenaline was coursing like fire in their veins. Kyle swiftly scooped up Jenna and ran with her in his arms. Chase, who was extremely fast for his age, and Vada kept up with Kyle. The people they heard across the clearing were now on their tail. She could hear them crashing through the forest behind them. The kids ran and ran, but fatigue was quickly setting in, especially for Vada, who was not a sporty person, unlike Kyle, who was a star running back of their football team and the region, and unlike Jenna, the best soccer player her age in the county, or Chase, who was on his way to becoming the fastest kid his age to run a mile in the state.

Vada decided to see who was chasing them. She turned her head.

It was like all the snow in the area had been dumped on her and all her muscles forgot how to move. Chasing them was half a dozen people dressed in red uniforms exactly like the ones in her dreams. She stopped running and started panicking. She felt like she was going to pass out. It was unbelievable and surreal.

"Vada!" Kyle screamed from several yards ahead. Vada took a deep breath and began sprinting again. But just like in her dream, it was no use. The soldiers were quickly closing in. Vada didn't see how they weren't going to get caught. Or worse, killed. Desperate groans were escaping her lips as she willed herself to go faster. The soldiers were right on their tails now.

Jenna screamed. There was a thud and a couple soldiers stopped running. Vada turned to see her little sister pinned under a soldier, who was unsheathing a sword.

"Jenna!" Kyle and Vada yelled in unison. They ran back towards her, towards the soldiers. Kyle tackled the nearest soldier who was too slow at reaching for his sword. Vada picked up a tree branch and wacked one against the head. They fell limp on the forest floor. Her next swing wasn't as lucky. The soldier stopped it with his sword and jerked it to the ground. Another soldier came up behind her and pinned her arms against her back.

She struggled and let out a cry as the other soldier raised his sword. The sound of something flying through the air caught the last bit of Vada's senses. She stood stunned as an arrow sunk deep into the chest of the soldier who was about to kill her. He fell lifeless. The soldier pinning her arms loosened his grip. She whirled around and punched him in the gut. He stood up and raised his fist. But some invisible force pulled her out of his range like in her dream. She watched in awe as a man dressed in fur clothes flew through the air at the man.

She crawled through the snow and jungle of people fighting. The soldiers were outnumbered by these strange people who came out of nowhere. The remaining soldiers fled, the one who had Jenna pinned down fled with a limp. Wait. Jenna! Vada stood up to run to her siblings, but was immediately assaulted by a large man dressed in dark fur, his face covered in black paint.

"Let go!" Vada screeched.

Her stomach dropped at the sound of Chase scream. It was from her right. A man was standing over him with a spear raised.

"Stop! Don't, please!" Vada screamed. The grip on her loosened. The spears were lowered. There were twenty-something people in fur in the area, and they were all staring at her. She took this moment to run to her little brother.

"Where are Kyle and Jenna?" Vada asked in Chase's ear as she hugged him. He was staring at her in bewilderment.

"Bring the others here," a deep voice commanded. It was the man with the spear. Jenna and Kyle were dragged out from behind bushes and dropped beside Vada. They all hugged each other tightly. Vada was relieved they were all alive.

"Who are you?" the man asked. His hardened face was looking at her very confused, and her siblings with rage.

With a shaky voice, Vada answered, "These are my—"

"I was asking the young man," the man boomed. Vada shut her mouth instantly and nudged Kyle.

"What?" Kyle asked through clenched teeth.

"He asked you a question and won't let me answer," Vada said.

"How am I supposed to know what he said?"

Vada looked at Kyle in unbelief. "What's that supposed to mean? He asked who you are."

"Vada, I can't understand him. He's speaking gibberish."

The look of rage grew as the man's patience shrank.

"Off with them," the man commanded.

Cold fear coursed through Vada.

"Wait!" she shouted. "Please. We aren't from around here. He can't understand you."

"Because he is one of them."

"What? One of who?"

The man scowled.

"Who are you?"

"Me? I—I'm Vada. Vada Rivka Jessica Thomas." Vada blurted. She didn't know why she said her full name or if she should have even said it. Three men were still aiming their spears at Kyle, Jenna, and Chase.

A murmur broke out when she said her name. She tried to hear what they were saying, but some words she didn't understand. Another thing she didn't understand is how she could even speak whatever language this was. If Kyle couldn't understand, then how could she?

The man called over another and whispered something to him. The smaller man nodded and took off through the forest. The large man turned back to Vada. "You all will come to our camp."

"All four of us?"

He nodded—with a glance of disgust at Vada's siblings-and motioned for them to stand. Vada did so and her siblings followed suit. Then they followed him through the forest, the other men following in defensive positions. For about an hour they trudged through the forest. Kyle kept a protective eye on his younger siblings, holding onto their arms or hands for a couple minutes at a time.

"Are we there yet?" Chase whispered. He was blue all over and shivering violently.

"I have no clue, bud," Vada answered. She bent down to rub his arms but the grunt of one of the fighting men had her moving again.

As they walked, little tents dotted the wooded landscape. The farther they walked, the more tents appeared closer together. The group entered little communities with more and more people and tents. The people ogled and pointed at Vada's siblings. They hiked up a mountain with camouflaged homes until they finally reached a wooden gate. The leader knocked on it three times. It opened a moment later and they entered. Large wooden buildings lined the street. People milled around, pointing at Vada's siblings like the people outside the compound did.

A couple dozen yards from the gate they entered a large square building. It had a sign over the door with some type of writing over it, but Vada couldn't read it. As they entered, warmth hit Vada like a smack in the face. It stung her frozen skin, but as she melted, she was grateful. A woman with poofy hair like Vada's walked up to the man. They kissed each other's cheeks.

"Visitors. Fetch them some clothes?" the man said. The woman nodded cheerfully and scurried out of the room. He turned to the kids and motioned them to follow him through the house. They walked through a couple rooms before sitting on the two couches in a sitting room.

The man just stared at them. He inspected each detail of

their appearances. Vada felt like he was staring at her for forever. His stare was starting to itch. Kyle scooted closer to Vada, squeezing Jenna and Chase between them, and put a comforting hand on her shoulder. Luckily, the woman came back with bundles of cloth a moment later.

"Put these on in the next room. You can leave your clothes in there. Then come back in here," the woman said compassionately. Vada nodded and walked out of the room, her siblings right on her heels. Once they were all in the empty room, Kyle shut the door.

"What are we doing. Putting these clothes on?" he asked.

"Yeah. Everyone just go to a corner and don't look. Stay there until we're all done changing," Vada said. So they did. Vada was relieved to slip out of her cold, wet summer clothes and into warm, dry winter clothes, though the material was a bit itchy.

"Vada, how come you look like everyone here?" Chase asked in a small voice from his corner; his voice couldn't hide the fact that he was still freezing cold. Vada thought back to everyone she had passed; they were all tall with dark complexions, dark hair, sometimes with poofy afro hair like hers, and with gray eyes.

Vada sighed and answered, "I don't know. Coincidence probably."

"Well then how come you can understand what they say? To me it sounds like dsgfbsinkhdfbe," Jenna said. Everyone chuckled, but there wasn't real happiness. There was no denying that everyone was scared out of their wits.

Vada already asked herself how she could understand this foreign language and got no answer. It was weird, everything that was happening. She looked like these people, understood most of what they said, saw the red soldiers from her dreams, and had that sense of belonging.

"Everyone done?" Vada asked, ignoring Jenna's inquiry. Everyone said yes and they walked to the middle of the room.

"I'm scared," Chase whimpered. Kyle pulled him into a big bear hug and rubbed his back.

"It's alright, bud. We're gonna be okay. I promise," Kyle responded. He looked up at Vada. It was hard to tell behind his mask of fearlessness, but Vada knew he was just as scared and lost as their nine year old brother.

"What about Mommy and Dad?" Jenna squeaked.

Vada threw an arm around her little sister's shoulders. "I'm sure they're fine. We'll find them. Don't worry."

"How?!" Jenna crowed.

Vada kissed the top of her head in response.

"Let's get back in there before they pull their spears on us again," Vada suggested, letting go of Jenna and walking to the door.

As they walked to the sitting room, Vada couldn't help but feel like she was in charge. Vada thought she was acting just as their mom does when they get lost on a road trip or something. If their parents weren't around, Kyle was usually the one who bossed everyone around. Vada usually did as everyone said. She guessed the language barrier was what was demoting Kyle's leadership.

The man and woman stopped talking when the kids walked in. They sat on a couch across from the one the kids had sat on. For some reason, Vada felt like she was walking into the principal's office.

When they sat down, the man spoke. "I am Jad. This is my wife, Nalania. Your names?"

"I'm Vada. That's my older brother Kyle and my younger

sister and brother, Jenna and Chase," Vada answered with a quiver in her voice.

Jad looked at Kyle sternly. "Does the young man not speak for this clan?"

Kyle was somewhat deflated under the stare, but reached his arm across the backs of his siblings again, squeezing their shoulders as he reached across. It was comforting.

"Um, well, you see, he can't speak... whatever language this is," Vada said.

Jad cocked his head to the side in confusion. Nalania smiled sweetly, but Vada could tell she was confused. What were they confused about? It's pretty obvious the Thomas kids had no clue what was going on.

"Where do you come from?" Jad asked.

"Um, we're from LA. In California. I'm not sure if you have ever heard of it," Vada answered.

Nalania perked up. "California! That's the place they took the—"

"Yes, Nala. Keep calm. We can't be sure," Jad interrupted.

"Oh....you're no fun," Nalania said, playfully smacking Jad's arm. Vada cocked her head. What was that she said? Oh well. All Vada really wanted to ask was what California meant to them and what was taken there, but she held her tongue. Societal rules were obviously different here, and Jad wasn't too happy Vada was doing all the talking. She guessed it was like pre-1920s America in this world where men were always in charge.

There was a loud knock at the front door. Nalania jumped up and ran to get it. Jad continued to stare at the kids, now thoroughly inspecting Vada. A few moments later, Nalania entered with the man who was sent away in the forest, a man in a navy uniform like those in her dreams, an old man, a young man a little older than Kyle, and a little boy. Jad stood up and high fived each person, though the high fives where chest high and super formal—except for the little boy. Jad gave him a scruff on the head. Vada guessed this was how these people greet each other. The Thomas kids were looking at the men in bewilderment at their greetings. Vada tried not to laugh at their expressions. Nalania pulled out some chairs for the men and the boy across from the couch the kids were sitting on.

"What is this about, Jad? Why do you have Mirrites here, in the compound?" the man in navy asked. Mirrites? What's a Mirrite?

"The girl says they are from California," Jad replied. Like Nalania, each of the men perked up and glanced at the kids.

"What are you doing with light-skins, girl?" the old man asked gruffly.

"Because they're my siblings," Vada responded, though it came out sort of like a question.

"And their names?" the old man asked in a husky voice.

"Ky—" Vada started but was cut off by the man sent away in the forest.

"You were not asked!"

Vada gulped and sunk down in her seat. Kyle's face grew red with anger, but Vada shook her head at him, as if saying 'Don't do anything.'

"Kyle, Jenna, Chase, and Vada. Vada Rivka," Jad said. The men's eyes widened. They all then huddled and started whispering so quick Vada couldn't catch what they were saying.

"Vada, what are they saying?" Jenna asked, her voice barely audible.

"I'm not sure."

The huddle broke and the man in navy started walking over

to Vada, the others watching anxiously. As he came closer, Vada thought he looked familiar, but she didn't know why.

"Hey, now, man," Kyle said in a gruff voice, squeezing Vada's shoulder harder than she would have liked.

"Stand," he commanded, ignoring Kyle. Vada did after a moment, and her siblings, not knowing what was going on, followed suit. The man in navy gave them looks of disgust, the only looks they have received since coming to this world.

"You all sit down," Vada commanded.

"Oh, okay," Kyle said. They sat down, their faces burning red.

"Stupid Mirrites," the man grumbled.

"Hey! They aren't Mirrites, or whatever that is. They're from California. We're from California," Vada snapped. She immediately started blushing at talking like that to a grown up. To her surprise, the shadow of a smirk appeared on his face. He then proceeded to stare at Vada, at her face mostly. Into her eyes, at her lips, her cheeks, her ears, even her hair.

"Is it her?" the young man asked after five minutes of inspection.

The man in navy smiled. "I think it is, Alakic."

"You sure?" Jad asked. He was smiling, too. In fact, everyone was smiling except Vada and her siblings.

"Who are you talking about?" Vada asked.

"There are too many links to deny it. The place, the age, the personality. And look at her! It must be her," the old man croaked.

"Hello?" Vada said impatiently. She didn't care how old they were or what society rules there were, she wanted to know what was going on.

"It is," the man in navy said confidently.

Nalania gasped. "Princess Vadalis!" The woman ran over

and pulled Vada into a tight hug. Vada went stiff. What? "You've come home! The...has been ....We're saved!"

Nalania spoke a bit of gibberish.

"The what has been what?" Vada asked, baffled by the hug and by the gibberish.

"The...has been ...! It's great!" Nalania yelled with excitement.

Vada was still confused. "I...I have no idea what you said. I'm sorry."

Nalania's arms dropped. "Oh." There was a crack in her voice. Her face suddenly lit up again. "That's okay! We can teach you! And your family!"

"I will not have Mirrites learning our language. They could spy," Jad growled.

"What is a Mirrite? Whatever it is, I can guarantee that my brothers and sister aren't it. They're from California! And I am too! What do you mean I came home?" Vada said in exasperation.

"Do you not remember? You are Princess Vadalis of Leaban! We were attacked and enslaved by the Mirrites twelve years ago. You were three when the attack on the castle happened. Most of our people, your people, were either killed or taken from our homeland and enslaved here, in this icy northern land. The queen made me save you by sending you to another world right before she died. You don't remember that?" the man in navy explained.

Vada let his words sink in. Most of what he just described was exactly how her dreams played out. Could what he says be true? How could it? She was from California, the only home she's ever known. Her parents were Tyler and Vanessa Thomas, the only parents she's ever known. But then again, she remembered struggling in early elementary school, struggling to communicate with other kids and to learn how to read. And she did look an awful lot like these people and very unlike her family. The more she thought about it, the more tears built up in her eyes and ragged her breathing got.

"I'm going to need a minute," Vada choked. She quickly stood up and ran into the other room, where they had changed clothes. As soon as she shut the door, tears spilled onto her cheeks. She let out a sob, but covered her mouth when she heard how loud it was. She slid down the wall and cried into her knees. The door opened quietly and someone slid down beside Vada. They put their arms around her and rubbed her back while she cried. It was Kyle. The back rubbing was his signature move.

When her throat loosened, Vada spoke with cracks in her voice, her head still in her knees. "Why didn't anyone tell me I was adopted?"

Kyle was silent for a moment. He cleared his throat and replied, "Sis, we—they promised me not to tell until they told you when you were sixteen. They were literally about to tell you on your birthday next month."

"Why couldn't y'all tell me earlier?"

"I don't know. You know how our parents are sometimes. Very stingy about certain stuff. I was five and just excited to 'buy' a sister." This drew a chuckle from Vada and she lifted her head.

"Did they know where I came from?"

"No. You kind of just appeared at the orphanage and they wanted you. We were all really excited. We were warned you were foreign, though they didn't know your background before you got there."

Vada took a deep breath. After a moment, she stood up,

ready to go back in the sitting room. "Do you think they knew I was royalty?" Vada asked with a chuckle.

"What? You're royalty? Since when?" Kyle balked.

"Oh yeah. Forgot you can't speak... whatever it is. Well, come on. Let's figure out what the heck to do now." Vada said with a smirk, throwing her arm behind Kyle's back, and his arm over her shoulders.

When they entered the sitting room, they were met by Nalania and the little boy playing some handshake game with Jenna and Chase.

"Vada! Look what they taught us!" Jenna said excitedly before demonstrating the handshake.

"Cool!" Vada said before turning to the men who were yet again huddled together. She cleared her throat in an authoritative way. If she really was a princess, the action felt right. The men stopped slowly and turned to look at her.

"Princess Vadalis. Is everything alright?" the young man asked when none of the older men said anything.

"Um, yeah. I was just needing some clarification. You all seem pretty certain I'm this long-lost princess. I'm pretty certain I have no clue what's going on. Can you catch me up?" Vada replied, throwing back her shoulders to make herself seem taller. For a moment, she thought the men would be angry. Then they all broke into smiles and began talking excitedly.

They repeated some of what they said: their country; Leaban; being invaded and conquered; the people being enslaved; her parents trying to run away during the attack; Vada being given to the man in navy to save her. What was interesting was that the uniformed man, Jerem, was something called a World Hopper, or someone who could "jump" from world to world. It was a very rare gift only held by Leabans because of a special plant in their country. The Mirrites, the people who conquered Leaban, still hadn't been able to find this special, power-giving plant.

Since the Leabans have been forced to Mirr, along with several other countries, a resistance has been building. There are many small resistances all around Mirr, each conquered country having its own; Leaban had the strongest. The leaders of the resistance were working together to plan and find ways to claim their freedom and destroy the Mirrites. However, the Mirrites were obviously very strong, smart, and deadly.

"But now we have an advantage over them. Not only do we have a resistance leader," the young man, Alakic, said, pointing his thumb at Jad, "but we also have royal blood!"

"What does that have to do with anything?" Vada asked in a shaky voice. All this talk about conquering people and destroying them was freaking her out.

"It would take a while to explain, but trust me. They would have a much harder time against us with you helping us." Jerem said.

"Helping you? Helping you do what exactly?" Vada said in exasperation.

In the corner of her eye, she saw Kyle perk up at her sudden rise in volume and change in mood. She let out a deep breath and rephrased her question in a calmer tone.

"Well, you'll help us conquer the Mirrites of course and help us get back to Leaban and retake our country. And as courtesy, we'll help the other countries retake theirs as well," Jad explained like it was supposed to be obvious.

"I—I never—no. I—I can't do that. I just want to get my parents back and go home." Vada's voice rose again.

"Vada? What's going on?" Kyle called from across the room. She ignored him and focused on the men in front of her.

"I knew it. She's too young," the old man, Cheeng, grumbled.

"What were we thinking? She hangs out with light-skins!" Smahel, the warrior sent away in the forest, spat.

"Can I talk to you privately, please?" Vada asked Jad desperately, starting to falter under all the exasperations and stares from everyone. Jad nodded and quietly led her out of the room, down the hallway, and into a room. It must be his office. Jad motioned for Vada to sit in one of the chairs surrounding the large table in the middle of the room.

"What is this about? You can't help us? Why not?" Jad asked. He sounded slightly angry, but calm at the same time.

"Listen. I just got here, learned I'm from a different world, learned I'm a princess, and now am expected to help fight a whole army and travel across several countries. Not to mention I almost died, like a lot! Can you understand why I'm being hesitant?" Vada explained quickly.

Jad was silent for a minute, contemplating what Vada said.

"So tell me about your parents."

"What do you want to know? All you need to know is that they were taken by the Mirrite soldier people in the woods and I want them back."

"How can you be sure they are alive?"

Vada's jaw dropped. "Oh my gosh! That's—I don't know. I mean, I'm sure they're alive. They have to be. And I'm not going to help anyone until I know they are alive and they're back with me and my siblings."

Vada was shocked at her defiance, but didn't let it show. She stared hard at Jad.

"Princess, we need you. You are the key to freeing our people—your people—and many other innocent people. We need you," Jad said in what sounded like a pleading voice, though it was hard to tell through the deep, gruffness.

"The only people I want to free right now are my parents."

For several minutes, the two went back and forth. Jad wanted Vada to stay and help the resistance conquer the Mirrites and retake their country, Leaban. Vada wanted to rescue her parents and get her family back to California. They compromised on saving her parents, but everything was still in the air. And they were getting nowhere.

"Fine. If you won't help us save the people, then we won't help you get your parents back," Jad growled.

"What? No! Having you guys help would be the only way I could get them back!" Vada screeched.

"Quiet down, Princess. There's no need to shout. I'm not budging. If you want your parents back, you will help your countrymen and save your people. It is your duty."

Vada buried her face in her hands. She was exhausted and arguing with a grown man about the fate of her parents was not making matters any better. Vada sat like that for a while, contemplating everything. For all she knew, she might not even have to really do anything to overtake the Mirrites. And she just wanted her parents back. And so did Kyle, Jenna, and Chase. Her parents were their biological parents after all. And if she helped them and got her parents back, she might get to go back home once it's all over, back to California. Nothing was making much sense in her exhausted state except the repeating fact that she needed to rescue her parents. The only way that was happening was to help the resistance and "her people." That was weird to think about. Ruling people.

Vada let out a long sigh and looked back up at Jad, who was studying a paper on the table. She sighed again, getting his attention.

"So?" Jad asked, folding his hands together.

"If I help you overtake the Mirrites, save everyone, and get back Leaban, you're saying I'll get my parents back and go home? "Vada asked, rubbing her tired eyes.

Jad hesitated before replying, "You'll have to receive some training. And we will have to teach you and your siblings things that you will have to do. You will also be a part of a campaign with the resistance and in strategy."

"So is that a yes?" Vada said impatiently.

Jad nodded. "Yes. If you help us, we'll get your parents back."

Vada let out a sigh of relief. Finally, after the longest day she has ever endured, after multiple life and death situations, after learning so many things about her past, after learning what was expected of her now, and knowing the safety of her and her family was taken into account, she could breathe freely.

"So when do we begin?" she asked, pulling her shoulders back, confidence and authority filling her up.

Jad smiled in appreciation.

"Tomorrow."

THE EARTH

By Kierstin Prentice

THE EARTH IS NOT FRAGILE
    Plants grow back after tornadoes
    Earthquakes
    Hurricanes
    Volcanic eruptions
    The sea is unpredictable and untamable
    Lightning bursts and thunder roars
    The Earth has the ability to kill

The Earth is not fragile
    But we have destroyed Her
    We have torn down
    Millions upon millions of trees

Without replacing any
We have hunted animals to extinction
Without a single thought
We have poisoned Her, we have bombed Her
We have over-populated Her and polluted Her
The Earth is not fragile
We are killing Her
And She is disintegrating.

THE ANGEL WITHOUT WINGS

By Anna Frazier

A LITTLE GIRL LAYS IN A HOSPITAL BED KNOWING TODAY would be her last. The girl's name is Angel, she looks over at her mother who's still in tears from the news that the doctor has given just minutes ago. "Mommy, what will happen to me after I die?" Angel asked her mother, tears about to flow from her own eyes. Her mother's eyes widen from shock at the question. She sniffled, starting to cry even more, "You will go to heaven, of course, where angels belong." Angel couldn't understand this. How could she get to heaven without wings? All angels had wings except her.

Tears started to run down little Angel's cheeks and the rain started to pour down as if the sky was crying with her. Thunder crackled across the dark night sky right before Angel cried out to her mother, "And how am I supposed to get there? I don't have wings like the rest of them!" Her mother jumped up, and told her child, "Don't worry, for you will be blessed with your own wings when it's time." Angel worried about not being able to make it to heaven. Her mother worried how she will make it without her personal angel. Even though she knows her Angel is needed in heaven, for she wouldn't be called there unless she was needed, and that must be why the child wants to go. She knows deep down her own purpose.

The mother has been blessed to have given birth to an angel, even if the angel child could only have stayed with her for a short while. The mother watches her child's tears turn into ones of happiness, so she forces a smile. The little girl softly tells her mother, "I hope you're right, because they've come for me...." The mother forces her smile to stay, because she wants her little Angel to remember her mother happy for her. Happy for her to go where she truly belongs: with the other Angels.

The mother has no doubt in her mind that is where she's going, because she is a real angel. The heart monitor beeps and her mother falls to her knees, crying. She just lost her only child, her angel. Once she is able to pull herself together enough to stand, she does so. She looks down at the dead child to see a white feather on her chest. Some might think the feather was from the pillow, but the mom knew the truth. This feather was left by her Angel as if to tell her mother she was right. The mother whispers quietly, "I told you. I told you that you would get your wings. Now you can live in heaven forever, Angel."

FORBIDDEN

By Vesta Dennis

THE ROOM IS FILLED TO THE BRIM WITH PEOPLE OF ALL ages and social statuses. Each person sits anxiously in rows leading to a pedestal sitting next to a platform where two people are standing.

In each corner of the room sits the accused, Alden and Sasha, who are thought to have a relationship. A relationship that brings them to this room; one that will decide the end of this trial that could snuff out their lives. Augustine, the old man in black formal robes stands on the pedestal, while the other, Jekyn, stands to the right wearing a brown overly-priced suit.

"Will Katherine Mar come to the front please," a voice commands which would normally be presented as an invitation by Jekyn. Everyone know he hates humans which means this will not end well for the woman. It also means he will not be so cordial towards Katherine for her obvious sympathy towards humans. What no one knows is Augustine is after Alden's position of power. He is here to guarantee—even if he cannot take him out—that Alden will not be able to maintain his throne.

Katherine stands in front of the crowd. Long brunette hair flows down her sides in waves. She wears a thick crimson apron over a simple, beige dress covered in mud at the hemline. She's small enough to be mistaken as a child, not an adult. Her walk is excruciatingly slow for the audience who are impatient to see the results of the trial.

"Could you tell us what the relationship between this human and Alden is, Katherine?" Jekyn asks.

Katherine shifts slightly on her feet, glancing at the wall. The audience assumes it's due to the revulsion she feels about the possibility of their relationship being of an intimate nature. She only hates the thought of it ending with the couple's pain.

"Katherine, you are Alden's servant, so you would know more about him than others. Would you please tell these people what their relationship was? Remember, lying is forbidden, and in this case will cost you your life," Jekyn remarks with a smirk.

Katherine glances at Alden. He doesn't fret over what his servant will say, he knows she'll say what she has to, whether she wants to or not. He only hopes this doesn't have to end badly for her. He nods at her, giving permission. She falters in response then starts, "Originally, Alden and Sasha—" but is interrupted by Jekyn.

"We do not need the name of the human," he says as the room's silence rises to a whisper.

Katherine leers at Jekyn. "Alden and Sasha," she repeats sternly, emphasizing Sasha's name, "started off as slave and master as seen by outsiders, however, I doubt it even began as such. When he went to the market, he was only there to pass the time. There was no intention of actually buying anything, only to amuse ourselves with the stores' products. As we walked the streets, an auction was going on for a human who was 'of the best breed; beautiful and obedient.' We passed by with him showing no intention of bothering with it, that is, until he saw her. Anyone who witnessed their first meeting, would have known exactly what she was to him. He began making bids which eventually ended up being the highest bids I had heard of."

"Could you put clearly what the human is to him?"

"Sasha is Alden's mate." Katherine admits, leaving the room erupting in murmurs. Astonishment ripples through the room; relationships between the races are taboo, and entirely unheard of. A human and a werewolf in an intimate relationship is nothing more than salacious gossip—usually.

Since it's forbidden, there are certain procedures that people go through to change humans in any case a werewolf prefers them, though there has never been a case of a person born human being fated to a born werewolf; humans are more entertainment or pets; there for amusement. They have to go through a series of trials which will show how qualified they are to be a werewolf. If they complete the trials, they are bitten. If not, the human dies and the werewolf would move on.

Before the trial, Alden considered the change, but two concerns still haunt him: if Sasha died during the trial, or from being bitten.

Even though the trials are used to show their ability to with-stand transforming, it didn't give a guarantee the person bitten would survive. The survival rate is about fifty-fifty, which was too high of a cost for Alden to consider.

Alden eyes Sasha at the other end of the room. He expects to see fear in her eyes, humans aren't treated very well and how could he possibly hold that against her? However, what he finds isn't fear, but confidence.

She faces those who are judging her—judging them—unafraid and without a care of what they'll do to her. Alden recognizes the heavy feeling in his chest as defeat, he had given up. But, staring at her defiant expression, warmth wells in his chest as courage builds for him to face the ending, it doesn't matter what those filling this courtroom think.

Alden locks eyes with Katherine who is staring at him. They are both in pain, and they cannot deny their fear, but they are in this together. He smiles, pulling from Sasha's courage to give Katherine the encouragement to do what she must.

She turns to look at Augustine pointedly, "There is nothing wrong with what they have. We all hope to find our mate, and just because his happened to be someone who was born human doesn't mean he did something disgusting." Katherine turns toward the crowd of discontented faces and growing rumble of voices. No one likes what she has said; people stand, yelling obscenities about how odious Alden was for even accepting a relationship with a human.

"Silence!" Augustine yells, fighting for control. He grabs his gavel and slams it onto the desk, loud enough to scare the room to silence. He sneers at Katherine as he tells her to step down. Just as she goes to step down, he adds, "And Katherine, you will pay for your insolence after we are done here." His words are slow, restrained.

She knows him, his anger, and his need for control, his vindictiveness. She knows what's in it for her, but that will be physical. What they are facing now is a larger issue. If she stays silent, she knows her actions are worse. She knows Alden and Sasha's love isn't wrong like she knows how to breathe; it's natural. If the group does not learn to adapt, then the society will implode and no one will realize it before it's too late. When

Katherine takes her final step, she is lead out of the room. The people stare at her while she is escorted.

When the doors close, Jekyn announces the next witness. "Next is Edmund Greene." He's hiding his rage as if it's invisible ink on paper. No one notices his eyes glaring at Sasha. Nor do they notice his animosity growing as he finds her staring at him with the exact same enmity.

Jekyn tears his eyes away from her, glancing back down at his paper as he quickly clears his throat. "So, as we were just told," he says slowly, careful not to break his facade. "This human and Alden were mates, is there any way for you to confirm this evidence?"

Edmund glares at Jekyn. "Everybody can tell they are mates at this point, anyone who is around Alden would have been able to tell you their bond." Hate drips from his voice. Edmund is a human slave and hates werewolves. His days are spent looking for anything he can use to ruin the first werewolf within his reach. He feels no bounds to anyone's pain but his own and he feels no obligation to truth. "I can tell you the two were in a relationship. Before the two were taken into custody, I caught them lying together in bed." His lips curl into a sneer as he watches the crowds reactions.

Gasps shatter the silence as a general upheaval takes over the courtroom. Hands fly to cover mouths, eyes are wide in disbelief, some even grasp their faces in horror and two forms slump in their seats from the shock. But there is no denying the anger that quickly follows. Amusements, pets, entertainment, even slavery are all acceptable. But never, *ever*, taking one to bed.

"What did you do when you discovered the nature of their relationship?"

Edmund eyes Alden, then smirks. "I quickly went to find

the authorities. I proceeded to tell them everything I had witnessed. When I finished, they went to his bedroom, finding the woman lying in his bed while he was bathing."

To everyone in the room, this is more than enough evidence to have both of them executed. The problem is, it wouldn't matter who saw what, Alden has the right to defend himself. Sasha won't be permitted because she isn't seen as a person, much like an animal.

Jekyn turns around to the crowd of people in the room. Many of whom are ready to have this finished, knowing exactly what is going on. Though they know what has to happen next.

"Alden Creighton, come to the stand." Jekyn says through gritted teeth. The knowledge that Alden is intimate with a human makes him as low as one, therefore, he will be treated as such, despite Alden being perfectly able to kill him.

"As is stated in the law, you have a chance to redeem yourself. You may be able to tell us your side of the story, however, failure to do so, could result in the end of your life. Therefore, be careful in choosing your explanation, and/or evidence you wish to present to this room." Though this is explained to the room, no one will listen to Alden.

No one will believe him over the words of his servants and slaves. They are the ones in the house. They are the ones who knew him very well. His underlings know his secrets and they aren't afraid to tell.

"My only explanation to this ordeal is no one can choose who their destined one becomes, only fate; therefore, I have nothing to say to you except that Sasha is indeed my mate, and there is no one on this planet I would trade her for."

The room bursts into an uproar. Hands cover mouths and horror plasters across their faces.

Alden finds himself smiling. Nothing about this is funny,

but everyone's expressions amuses Alden. The way they're reacting reminds him of a small minded pigeon.

"So you have nothing to say to explain your situation with the human?" Jekyn protests.

"Absolutely not."

"Then," Jekyn begins, "we have no choice, but to place judgement."

Augustine clears his throat to declare his decision. "Alden, on accounts of your crimes, you and that human," he points towards Sasha with a thin finger while Alden stares him down, "are to be executed. Due to the extreme nature of your crimes, you both will be burned at the stake until you are presumed dead."

Jekyn's lips twist into a smile while Alden glares at Augustine. He knew his punishment would be death as well as Sasha's, but this is cruel. He hadn't thought Sasha would have to suffer during it. From the beginning he knew he was going to be caught, he didn't think she'd have to pay for it. Now there isn't anything holding any of them back.

"Your sentence shall be carried out today at sun down on the terms that you chose to be with a human despite our strict rules against them. Your human will be burned first while you watch. So, even in your afterlife you understand the weight of your crime."

Never in their history has there been an execution like this, nor in such a short time span. But the crowd doesn't register this fact. They feel the punishment is just because their hate for humans.

At sun down Alden and Sasha are tied to their posts, facing

each other. Sticks lay at their feet inside a ring of dirt. Everyone from the earlier trial, with the addition of others, stand watching their end.

Jekyn and Augustine stand side by side in front of the pair facing the crowd of people. "Now, as you all have heard, Alden has committed the worst crime of our kind." A pause. Then louder, "he pursued a relationship with a human."

Alden peers over the crowd of people *if only I had done something*. He believes there could have been something done about the way they perceive humans as useless, vial, repulsive, abominable things. If only he had shown them humans are very similar to werewolves, then this wouldn't have happened.

A man dressed in all black approaches the two with a torch in both hands. He touches the flames to the pile of wood at Sasha's feet.

As the fire burns closer, a crippling agony rises in Alden's chest. His heart slams wildly in his chest.

The fire lick at Sasha's feet and her screams pierce the night.

To this, Alden's heart clenches as if it were about to burst. This is excruciating, just as Augustine has intended. Nothing he has experienced in his life can amount to the helplessness, the pain, the failure he feels. The fire roars, consuming everything in seconds but it feels like hours until her screams stop. Alden welcomes the stranger in the black. This is his only escape from this agony. The flames will mean nothing because he has already lost a piece of himself.

"This is not the end," Alden whispers inaudibly. He repeats his words again, louder so everyone can hear him. The stranger touches the flames to the sticks at his feet. No one takes his threat seriously, but his words resonate deep within the crowd.

When the fire reaches Alden, he does not scream, only

closes his eyes tightly as if willing himself to sleep. His time is finished.

Those watching feel their emotions torn. This was one of their own but he betrayed them. What they don't understand is the feeling that keeps them from smiling is the discontent at the injustice that will engulf them in the most ruthless war their society has ever known.

SLEEPLESS NIGHTS

By Chase Harp

ON A NIGHT THAT MOST WOULD CALL THE PERFECT NIGHT, the sky was littered with stars and it was about 70 degrees with a slight breeze. I was driving like I usually did.

The windows were rolled all the way down and Queen was blasting through the speakers. I was clearing my head after having a hard day at work. Life up to this point had been amazing in the sense I was still alive and I had plans to make something out of myself, but the one thing I had always wondered was if love was ever real and with being 17 I knew that I knew nothing about it like everyone else my age did or so I thought.

I was cruising going about 70 down back roads and suddenly I saw lights from nowhere on the opposite side of the road and *bam!* Both mine and the others car's fenders were torn to shreds I came to a screeching stop and jumped out to see if my car was ruined. Once I realized I had totally messed my car up I noticed the other car had stopped so I started my way to it.

I could tell by the body style it was a blue 2015 Dodge Dart and as I was making my way to the car I was thinking about what I was going to say as I did with every conversation. I was scared to the point where I was as pale as the moon. I had never been in an accident involving another person. As I got about 100 feet away from the other car the door swung open with a sense of authority like the person opening it was important and they had entitlement issues.

"Umm, are you uhh, okay?" I asked, clearing my throat trying to make it sound as if I was confident in what I was saying.

And the voice that replied had seemed almost angelic and heavenly.

"Oh my God, are you okay? I'm fine." There she stood, the moonlight shining off her long red hair and her green eyes seemed to brighten the night. She was tall, toned, and beautiful. Nothing like I had ever seen before as I stood there at a loss for words being star-struck by the beauty I was witnessing on this forever magical night. She started towards me and I started to stutter as I always do when I'm nervous or excited.

"I-I-I-I'm fine but I can't say the same thing about my car." I finally mustered up those words and it seemed like that's all I could say at that moment until I came to the realization that I was staring at her. She walked up to me and stuck her hand out.

"Hello, my name is Emma. It's a pleasure to meet a person who looks as well as you do after having their car ruined like that."

I shook her hand eagerly, almost creepily. "I'm Kai and may I say holy hell you are one of the most beautiful people I have ever met." I laughed nervously and began to blush. I could feel my face getting red hot. "And thank you it was just a little fender bender it's not that bad." I smiled cheesily trying to play it off. She just laughed as if I was the funniest person to ever tell a joke.

She said, "Well Kai, I'm guessing we are gonna have to trade information."

I nodded. "I suppose we are and I guess us wrecking is lucky for me because I get your number." I snickered and smiled.

"Well, let me go write everything down and then I will meet you at your car." She said flirtatiously. As I was writing everything down. She walked up to my open door and I saw her in the dim light of my cab lights and my jawed dropped. While my mind was racing, I wrote down all my information that she needed. When I finally looked up I saw her walking back towards my car. I hopped out of my car and met her halfway so she didn't have to walk all the way back to my car.

She slowly talked as if to milk every moment with me. "I wrote everything down that you need to know, my name, my number and all other needed information...I assume you have done the same...?"

I nodded in agreement still shocked from seeing her. I handed her my information as she handed me hers I started to get cocky. " So, I wish I could've met you under different circumstances. I mean, this is not the greatest way to make a first impression. I ruined your ride."

She shrugged and replied with the same arrogance, "Well it's not every day that you get to meet an...interesting person such as yourself."

I smirked and giggled, "Is that so?" She nodded. "Can you still drive your car or can I take you somewhere?"

She seemed to think for a split second before making a

decision and finally said, "It will drive but I will keep that in mind that you owe me a ride. I will be in touch with you Mr. Kai."

She walked off immediately leaving me speechless and smiling like an idiot.

This was only the beginning of something that I was clueless was going to turn into something that would form the remainder of my life.

The next day I was hanging out with a bunch of my friends. They had come over to my house to see how bad the damage was on my car. My friend, Brennen, finally spoke up after we stood in awe of the car. "So what kind of person hit you at three in the morning Kai? Also, what the hell were you doing out at three in the morning in the first place?"

I snickered. "Bro, don't even worry why I was out at three in the morning I'm pretty sure we all know what I was doing." I smirked trying to gloat in front of my friends as I always did. "Anyway, the person that hit me was sent from up above. How about we all go to our secret spot to discuss this there, I just got some so we should roll up."

They all agreed so we piled into Brennen's car. There was Brennen, Alec, Matt and I. As we pulled up to the spot we had always hung out at which was often referred to as "Little Dixie," we got out and all sat on the hood of Brennen's car. I pulled out the stuff and started going into great detail about Emma. As I got done explaining her to them, Alec spoke up.

"There is no way that she is that pretty Kai. You have to be pulling our legs." He stated as smoke poured from his mouth. The guys continued to tease until finally I stood up getting defensive. "Guys, I'm being serious. There is no way that I could make this girl up. I didn't believe in love at first sight until I saw Emma." All of the sudden my phone started ringing. It was a number I had never seen before. I picked up after the third ring, "Go for Kai."

"Hey, it's Emma I wanted to ask if maybe sometime you and I could hang out. I'm pretty sure our parents got a hold of each other about our vehicles."

I was ecstatic and rapidly replied, "Hell yeah! When do you wanna catch up? I was speaking so fast that it seemed as if I was not breathing and with my friends making fun of me for how I was acting, I was already embarrassed and trying not to stutter.

She laughed softly, "Slow down there hoss cat and breathe. I was thinking Saturday night. You can pick me up at 9. I'll send you my address."

Immediately she hung up not giving me a choice to say no. I looked at my boys and smirked.

"Well boys, guess who has a date Saturday?" I put my arms up as they hyped me up. The days slowly passed until Saturday was finally here and I was freaking out. Dad even commented on it, calling me out, he laughed saying, "Kai I haven't seen you this worked up since you were trying to find a good way to tell me that you were sneaking out to parties on the weekends."

I snapped, "Dad, I'm nervous, this girl is one in a million."

He stood there wide-eyed. He knew it was hard for me to connect to girls, really being that I didn't have a mother or other female influences in my life.

He finally found the words, "Well bubba, sit down." I did as I was told, thinking that I was in trouble. He looked me in the eyes, and struggling with what he was about to say, "Son, I understand what you are going through right now and I know I am supposed to be here to guide you through everything in life, but this is one thing you have to do by yourself. I really hope that this relationship goes as well as you hope it does. However, I don't want you to be disappointed if it doesn't. First impressions can be deceptive." I could tell he was struggling with his words, but there was sincerity in his voice.

I sat there absorbing everything that Dad awkwardly told me. I nodded and got up hugging him tightly, "Thanks Dad, I really needed that." I stated as I glared at the clock.

I was sure to be prompt to her house and I got out of my car wearing my best pair of my darker jeans held up by my brown leather belt, while tucked in my jeans was my plain white shirt and completing my outfit with my grey vans. In my mind, I felt as if I belonged in Grease singing next to John Travolta. I nervously knocked on the door and just stood waiting. Her mother and father answered the door. In all honesty, I almost passed out from the shock and fear of meeting them for the first time. They smiled warmly and her dad said, "So you must be this Kai guy that we keep hearing about."

I stuck my hand out and smiled in relief knowing that I was someone that she was talking about regularly. "Yes Sir, I'm Kai Martin. It's a pleasure to meet you." They shook my hand and looked me up and down.

They called out, "Emma, Kai is here to pick you up." Then I saw her. She walked down the stairs in light blue jeans that showed off her legs which looked like a curvy back road. She had on a white crop top and wore high top black converses. Her long red hair was curly and placed in a ponytail making her bright green eyes seem to illuminate the room. In my mind, it seemed like she was walking in slow motion and suddenly she ran past me and grabbed my hand taking me outside.

She called out to her parents, "Bye Mom, bye Dad! I love you!" I smiled and let her drag me to my car. While buckling in, I broke the silence with, "You look stunning, might I say. Are you ready for the wildest ride of your life?"

She gave me a snarky smirk, "Lets go pretty boy." I nodded

and slammed on the gas in my dad's five speed Mustang causing the tires to start to squeal and spin. The cab of the car started to fill with the smell of burning rubber and we shot off like a rocket towards the back roads. With the windows down and wind whipping through our hair she said, "So tell me about yourself."

I smiled, replying quickly, "So I am basically just a fun loving guy that is just here for a good time not really a long time but in all reality I just want to make my Dad proud to show him I can be a good guy and shape up and become a real man"

She smiled warmly at my response and started talking about herself. "Well Mister 'have a good time,' I just moved here from the county over and you're really one of the first boys that I'm really meeting and may I say I am impressed." I started to blush and she looked at me seriously, "So what do you really do around here for fun other than just drive around?"

"Well you have to know people to have fun around here and I mean fun other than drinking and smoking. My friends and I typically explore the county and see what we can find that is new and exciting. Normally we go to mine or Brennen's house just hanging around listening to music. Normal teenage boy stuff, ya know."

"So basically, you all just party around here for fun, you don't do anything else?"

I stared at the road blankly as I pondered her question. "Well, I mean, we do have a hangout place where we tend to go fishing for fun. You wanna go there?"

Her green eyes seemed to catch fire. I smirked as I pulled the emergency brake immediately sending the car spinning in circles. Over my laughter I heard her screaming.

I could tell that she wanted to get in trouble with me. We came into the city speeding past cars. Then when I was stopped at a stop light, I saw them. Blue lights seemed to illuminate everything inside the car. Emma and I looked at each other. I couldn't tell if it was the look in her eyes or the nod that she gave me but after a second of seeing the lights, I dumped the clutch and took off once again. My heart was pumping as we sped away from the cop. He wasn't far behind me, basically nipping at our heels. We had finally made it out of the county once again and he was still on our heels thinking that he could catch us by himself. Suddenly I knew what to do. I laughed, "Hold on to your ass." I laughed as I cut the wheel sharply and she screamed while we cut through a cornfield and the cop didn't dare to follow. As we cut through the corn field it dumped us out on an old dirt road that I oddly knew where it was so I came to a shaking stop. Once I got the car stopped, I looked at Emma and laughed. We said in unison "Oh, my God that was fun!" I blushed as she leaned over and kissed my cheek.

"Why don't we just stay out of town for the rest of the night. They will be looking for us for a while so we better stay clear." I nodded in agreement.

"Yeah, my Dad is probably going to kill me for how dirty I got his car, but it was the only way I knew how we could get away." I smiled still being scared about the whole cop-thing, knowing that they were probably going to be waiting on me at my house and had already informed my Dad about what I did. However, at this moment I didn't care. I felt free and I had this girl sitting next to me. It was weird. She was with me, so I felt complete. I had never felt like this before in my life. As we finally got the nerve to actually drive again, we rode out to Little Dixie. We got out of the car and sat on the hood. We started casually talking, but it soon turned into an in-depth conversation. She hit me with a question that I wasn't prepared for, yet I replied so quickly and casually.

"Are you scared of death?"

"No, I don't plan on living past 21. I know I'm not right about it, but at the same time I know I'm not wrong."

She just sat there shocked staring at me, "Kai, is there something that you need to talk about?"

I just shrugged, "It's not that I need to talk about anything. I don't plan on living long; I want to live while I'm alive, so life is just pointless after that. Right?"

"Life isn't pointless. You complete one task and you move onto another. Do you at least believe in love at first sight?"

I sat there wondering my response for a moment. "I mean, I just think that it will come when it does...but I am starting to believe in love at first sight." She started to smile and quickly leaned in and kissed me. We deeply kissed for what seemed like forever and in that exact moment I knew, somehow that she was the one.

After she pulled away, she smiled softly saying, "I believe in love at first sight and I think I found one last night and he tends to drive very recklessly." I smirked.

"Yeah, I mean I actually am starting to believe that I could be a guy that would accept love at all."

Saying nothing, she just got up and grabbed my hand, pulled me off the car finally speaking. "I think you should be getting me home. After all, it is 4 in the morning."

"I mean I was having a good time but okay I can take you home." I opened her door for her and closed it after she got in. I walked to the driver's side of the car smiling like a dummy. As I got in I buckled up and looked over at her I said, "Get ready for another wild ride." As we pulled out, I spun my tires leaving black marks and we shot off like a dart in the night. Her parents were waiting on the front porch as we arrived she kissed me on the cheek and got out.

"Don't worry I'll handle them and I'll text you later," she stated as she walked toward her house.

I finally arrived home at 6 in the morning, I tried to sneak in, but as soon as the wheels of my car hit the gravel the blue lights of a cop car started to flash and my front porch light came on. There stood my Dad, and the cop that I had outran. I parked the car and started my way to them thinking to myself, *I can run away now and I can see her one last time before I'm grounded for life.* I stopped dead in my tracks and looked at the police officer and my father standing about 20 yards from me and I checked my phone. There was one text from Emma. "Come see me, it'll be the last time this summer. My window is the second one on the ground level in the back of the house." I smirked, knowing I was going to be in for a world of hurt. I started the car again and sped out of my driveway. Rushing to her house as fast as I could when I got there I didn't even bother to turn my car off. I just ran to her window, tapped on it lightly, and it flew open.

"Didn't think that you were gonna come over speed racer."

"I'm going to be grounded for life." I kissed her deeply and pulled away. "By the way, I'm in a ton of trouble, the police officer did not seem very happy as I pulled out of my driveway."

"Do I hear him in your room Emma?" Emma's dad yelled all of the sudden.

"No, Dad he isn't here!" She lowered her voice to a whisper. "Okay, you have to have to get going speed racer." She started pushing me toward her window.

Arriving at my house, another cop car pulled in behind me. I smiled and laughed, I turned the car off and threw the keys down on the ground and confidently walked up to my father. "Dad, let me tell you I regret nothing that I did tonight and I will suffer all the repercussions of it."

He stood there dumbfounded. "Well if you accept everything, then you are just grounded all summer and that means you are to be only here working or doing your community service these nice officers are about to tell you that you have to do."

The cop nodded and looked over to me, "Your father is right, son. You are lucky we are not arresting you right now. Next time you'll definitely be behind bars regardless of your father's status in our academy. So let's make sure there isn't a next time. You have a good 500 hours of community service to do so let's say we start Monday at 6 in the morning, bright and early." I nodded in response.

"Yes sir." I pushed past everyone and marched to my room. As I got to my room and got ready for bed, I texted Emma.

"I am grounded all summer and I have 500 hours community service."

"That's tough, speed racer. I just got grounded all summer and I got told I'm not allowed to be around you."

"Then may this be the first time I say I can't wait for school to start back up."

The summer went by as the court has planned for it to go for me. I was basically friendless and I was just working day in and day out. Most of the work that I was doing was my community service and that was easy. All I had to do was help take care of a farm which I had done my whole life. But the one thing I did find joy in during the summer was getting to text Emma. It had seemed that she and I had formed a bond. Yet we weren't dating. All we did was talk all night and it was normally through text, but on any given night you could find me talking to her on the phone. I sat around in my room putting my game on pause and making my online friends lose because I was talking to her.

The summer had fully passed and the next morning couldn't have come fast enough. When it did, I jumped up as my alarm went off. I was so excited I threw on my dark blue jeans that seemed to make my legs stretch forever and my plain black tee shirt that made my muscular body seem larger than it actually is. I threw on my brown leather jacket that seemed worn out but in all reality it was new. I just wore it so much it was in broke in. I also had my dark brown leather work boots on that seemed like they had seen hell and had come back with a new purpose. On the way to school I drove slowly as I was trying to think of the first thing I was going to say to her. It was weird I had waited all this time to see her and now it was close to time. I was at a loss for everything. As I pulled into the school parking lot I saw her car and I whipped my car in beside it quickly. I started to breathe slowly calming myself down. The next thing I knew, she was knocking on my window smiling. I got out of my car and checked her out, looking her up and down. She was wearing a yellow sun dress that seemed to bounce off her skin and it made her look downright beautiful. I smiled and leaned down and kissed her deeply, not saying a word. I didn't need words to say hello to her.

"So, Speed Racer, it looks like we have most of our classes together this year, so we have to make our last year amazing before you leave me for college." I just smiled and snickered pushing her slightly.

"It's not like I'm leaving forever. I'll be back after college. It's only 13 months." We walked inside the school flirting, bumping into each other, and holding hands. We got to our first class that we had together and we sat next to one another. I sat back in my chair.

"I think it's weird that we have never met each other until we had that wreck. I mean, we did go to the same school for 12 years," I said.

"You wouldn't want your life any other way now that I'm in

it," she sneered. I jumped back putting my hand on my chest acting like I was actually surprised that she had said that even though I had told her countless times that I would be lost without her.

The school year went on and life had been wonderful but there was something that was wrong even though nothing was being said. We could feel it growing between us. One day after school we were laying in a field across the road and she finally asked about it. "Kai, what is happening to us?"

I sat there shocked, even though I had been feeling it. I sat up, the cover sliding off my chest and I cleared my throat. "Well, I think it is mostly to blame on us doing all this college stuff. But, I mean, I don't leave 'til June, and I mean, it's only November so I don't find any need for us to worry just yet."

She just sighed and laid back down obviously not wanting to talk about the subject any more. I just rolled my eyes and laid back down covering up with my jacket and turning my back to her.

She looked at me while she was standing in front of my car's headlights and yelled, "You're leaving me Kai!"

I stood there stunned and I finally yelled back, "I'm not, I'm leaving for a year to make sure you have the life I feel like you deserve. I'm doing this all for you. No one else, just you. NOW THAT I HAVE YOU I ACTUALLY WANNA LIVE PAST 21. YOU'RE THE ONLY REASON Emma!"

"YOU AREN'T DOING THIS FOR ME. YOU'RE DOING IT SO YOU CAN LEAVE!" She dropped to her knees crying. I came over and held her as we sat in the middle of the road.

"Emma, I am doing this so I can make sure you have the life I want you to have. I am not going to forget about you. I can never forget about you. I love you and I always will. You are my first love and if things keep going at this rate you're going to be my only love until we have children."

She wrapped her arms around me. "You finally said it, I love you Kai." I sat there stunned. I had said it. Finally, after being involved with her, I told her my true feelings I had never told her. She looked up at me and I wiped her tears from her face.

"I've told you countless times I'll still come see you and you can come spend the weekends with me."

She sniffled "It's not going to be the same. That's why I think we need to break up."

I stepped back, stunned. My whole life for the past year was crumbling before my very eyes. It was like glass shattering. I said quietly, hurt, "What did you just say?"

"WE ARE OVER, KAI. WE ARE BROKEN UP!" She got up quickly and walked toward her car. I just stood there, dumbfounded. The girl of my dreams had just broken up with me because I was leaving to make better my life for her. I sat down in my car, broke down, and I started to cry. I was a grown man in my mind, yet I was in the fetal position, crying. I didn't know what to do until I finally drove home.

My Dad came to my car and all he said was, "I heard what happened, buddy. I'm sorry. Let me know if you need anything."

I got through school without hearing a word from Emma and even when I completed my degree from our local community college and moved back home I saw her around, but there were no words spoken between us. It was the worst feeling in the world and I regret it to this day. I miss her every day.

The love I found got taken away from me as quickly as it was given to me. She will never know all I have done from the time I met her, from the time she left me: it was all for her.

On my 21st birthday, I drove 120 mph with all of this in my

head, down the same back road where I had first met her, and flipped my car 8 times and got slung out.

I died instantly so I had no feeling of what it felt like—just how I felt without her. I know to this day that she blames herself, but it isn't her fault. In all reality, it is my fault. I got too attached to her and she got attached to me like we both never wanted, but it happened. I just want you to know I love Emma and I will continue to love her in this afterlife.

All I have to say Zeke, my dear brother, is don't make the same mistakes that I did when I was young. I was a dumb foolish kid that ended my own life just for a girl and I never want to see you do that. I want to watch you do something with your life.

Just know that I am watching over you and I always will be. Always stay strong for me and know I am in a better place with my mind and I can now see that there is more to life than just one silly girl. Life is all about working hard to enjoy the good that comes after. I found out if I had just waited and not been stupid, my life was about to get so much better. I had everything, and just threw it away because I let emotions take over. I'm sorry to you and to dad and to her. You deserve better.

STRAELINOR

By Jessica Smith

"Athena," I heard my father speak, pulling me out of my trance. "Look at me, my child." All demons served him as if he was the king of Hell. He ordered his demons to find me which they did. I looked down to see myself tied up, held tightly against the cold, metal chair by rope and demonic claws, the smell of death encircling the room. The metal along the walls let off a stench that mixed with the smell of rotting flesh, metallic, like iron. The wooden floors, rotting and falling under the structure of the abandoned church. If you weren't careful, you'd fall into one of the many holes already formed in the floor.

"No Father, I will never join the Satan of Straelinor." I felt my face heat up. I wanted nothing more than my family to be back together and happy. But father would never make that possible. He was set on punishing us hybrids. We call ourselves Numeorians, half fallen angel and half witch.

"Then you will suffer along with all Numeorians, your time will come." He turned around and walked toward the doorway, then he turned to get the attention of his demons before continuing out. The old wood creaked under the heels of his boots. With a flick of his wrist, the demons followed him out.

I struggled to free myself from the rope, being cautious of the noisy wood beneath me. My auburn hair fell into my face, blocking my view. As I twisted my wrist around trying to free it, burn marks from the rope appeared on my skin. I managed to loosen the rope from the struggle and pulled both of my wrists out. They were raw and I rubbed them softly, glad to have them free. I examined the room trying to find my Infamy, or otherwise known as a short sword. Infamy's are light weight weapons for Numerions like me. Most soldiers that fight in wars against the demons use Shadowsteel, otherwise known as a great sword.

I spotted my Infamy, thrown into one of the many holes that are in the church floor. I sighed and jumped in. Numerions have good agility and aren't easily breakable like mundanes are. We also have bracelets given to us during the ceremony that makes us official Straelinor demon hunters. The bracelets help us contain our magic. Since we have witch blood running through our veins, we needed something to help us access the power.

I picked up my Infamy, it felt lighter than normal. I tossed it through the hole and heard it clang against the wood. I put my hands against the wood (that was somehow still attached to the church) and pulled myself up, back into the room filled with the scent of rot. I grabbed my Infamy once again and headed out the door. I looked around the streets and sighed. Father had brought me to the town we once lived in when I was about seven years old. I rolled my eyes and began my journey back home, to Straelinor. Father used to hide me in the mundane realm so The Theocratic Brotherhood wouldn't find him.

The Theocratic Brotherhood is like the rule makers of our kind. They make laws to be sure we don't decide to kill the ones we've sworn to protect or each other.

I reached the building I had been looking for. It was a large, grey, beaten up house. Numerions used this house to teleport back and forth between the mundane world and Straelinor. Portals aren't fun to go through. They burn your lungs and it feels like you're suffocating, like your body is slowly filling up with water. It's one of the worst feelings we have to endure as our kind.

I sighed and opened the antique door to the building. Knowing I would dread every second of this, I closed my eyes and took a deep breath, then stepped through the door. As the portal bent and twisted my figure, the feeling of water engulfing me, I thought of home. The portal wouldn't work unless you had a specific location you wanted to reach. I thought of the creek that ran behind our house, the tiny waterfall that you can hear even while you're inside. The birds that chirped in the trees lining the water. I thought of my bed, comfy and cozy. There was nothing like sleeping in your own bed that was provided by your parents. It makes you feel safe, loved.

I gasped as I felt my feet land on the ground. They weren't there long because I fell on my back. I rubbed my eyes, trying to erase the pain of the journey. I coughed and pulled myself to my feet.

"Lily!" My little sister yelled in a high-pitched voice. She came running out of the door. Lily is my middle name, Julia found it easier to say than Athena. Her tiny shoes grabbed the dirt as she ran. She wrapped her arms around me and squeezed.

I coughed. She may be tiny but she's definitely strong. She would be carrying Shadowsteel one day.

I huffed and heard my mother hollering from the door. "Ath, where have you been?" She scolded. "Oh you know, kidnapped. Father thought he would take interest in me." I said sarcastically.

Her eyes suddenly grew wide and the thought of *him*. "Athena, stop. It's not funny. Isiah isn't a joke. He could've hurt you." She spoke in a soft voice, pretending she wasn't infuriated as she walked out of the door and over to me. She managed to get Julia off of me and took her place. The good thing about mom hugs is that they heal any wound, no matter how deep.

"I know, but he didn't. That's what matters." I said quietly as I hugged her back. I couldn't help but smile. Mom hugs are the best. After the day I had, I really needed the hug. I may be stubborn and held myself together, but that doesn't mean it didn't hurt.

"Good." She pulled away and smiled weakly at me. She grabbed my hand and pulled me up the ancient stone pathway leading to the house. I chuckled lightly and followed her through the old, oak wood door.

Almost instantly, my German Shepard jumped over the couch that was centered in the living area and ran over to me, knocking me off my feet. I let out a soft grunt as I hit the ground. "Stella!" I laughed as she licked me in the face. Someone cleared their throat from the dining room, to my right. I turned my head and spotted Lewis Grey.

I moved Stella to the side and pulled myself to my feet. Lewis will always will be my best friend. He was also a Numerion so I didn't have to hide from him, like I do with my mundane (full-blooded human) friends. We're supposed to keep mundanes in the dark about us and demons, but the full blooded witches like to make themselves obvious by telling them their future and fortune. If the mundanes were to discover us, they would start a war. That's how they always solve their problems, violence.

I swiftly ran over to Lewis and hugged him tightly, being careful not to knock him off his feet. Believe me, that floor was not comfortable. It was hardwood. Stella didn't even have the decency to knock me over on the carpet in the living room. Lewis chuckled and wrapped his arms around me, squeezing me like a child that he thought was lost forever.

"I guess you missed me." He let go of me and pulled away, looking at me. "Of course I did. You're my best friend. Plus, you've been training basically all day, every day. So I never get to see you." I laughed.

"That's true. I hate training. How did you get lucky enough to finish early?" He asked, walking out of the dining area and into the living room. He strode over to the dull, brown couch that Stella had claimed as hers when we got her. I pointed to my mom.

"Because of that woman right there. She started training me herself at an early age, so I skipped most of the classes you're taking right now." You're allowed to start training your children early so they can be in the battlefield sooner, but Lewis' parents decided against starting him early. I followed him over to the couch but was cautious enough to sit on the floor. I didn't want to be the one to upset Stella once she found out someone was in her spot.

Almost on cue, Stella ran into the living room, diving right on top of Lewis. He shrieked and got up, apologizing to her. I shook my head and stepped outside, breathing in the fresh air. Lewis followed me. I turned to look at him and gave him a smirk, taking off down the hill toward our secret hideout.

I dodged trees, bushes, logs, and other objects in the way. I slightly turned my head to the right and saw Lewis close behind me, which cause me to speed up. As I reached the end of the path we had created so many years ago (which the grass had grown back and covered again), I slowed down and came to a stop in front of the cave. The cave was shaped by the roots of a large tree and it went down into the ground, underneath of the tree. I climbed under the roots we had used to cover the cave. It's not a secret hideout if someone else finds it, right?

I looked around at several items we brought here as kids. Books, shelves, weapons, and some canned food that hasn't expired yet. I turned my head slightly to the right and spotted the wooden chair I painted purple when I was seven years old. I sighed and plopped down into it.

I heard twigs snap and leaves crunch as Lewis grew closer to the caves entrance. He was breathing heavily as if he had just been at the gym for hours. Compared to my mother and I, Lewis is out of shape. He hasn't been training to be a Straelinor soldier near as long as I have. He moved the logs and crawled down into the cave. He then pulled back the dark brown curtain we used to cover the opening, making it less noticeable to people passing by.

I tried not to laugh at the look on his face. He always won at races, but this time I was very far ahead. Numerions had super speed, but not like vampires you read about in stories. We weren't vampires but we did have a couple traits that resembled them. We were just faster than the average mundane. As Numerions, we were part human as well; Considering witches were mundane at one time. Most of all, I enjoyed the running part of my training. It made me feel free, like I was untouchable. The speed, the wind, the sound of leaves rushing under my feet. It's all an incredible experience that's better to do than say. "You finally caught up. I guess you're getting slower." I smirked at my best friend who didn't seem very amused.

"Or you're just getting faster." He finally caught his breath and sat in the blue chair beside my purple one. Lewis had painted the blue one when I did the purple. "Hungry?" He asked and picked up a can of fruit. He grabbed the can opener from the shelf beside it and swiftly sat back down. The shelf with all of the food was right beside Lewis' chair. All of this felt nostalgic. I laughed quietly and nodded my head as he opened the can and handed me a plastic spork.

Suddenly, we heard footsteps outside of the cave. Both of us froze, unable to move. My mother said she was going to tell the Theocratic Brotherhood about my father floating around again. So with the alarm about my father going around Straelinor, it could be anybody. My father's army could've easily followed us without us seeing or hearing them. The footsteps stopped right in front of the cave. My eyes became devilish looking as I thought about attacking them, knocking them out. I looked at Lewis and he shook his head as if to say it was a bad idea. I stood up anyway and peaked through the curtain, just barely.

My breath caught. A demon. One of my father's. Once one demon saw the hideout, so would the rest. Their sight could connect so that if one of them were to see an important location, the rest would know it as well. It kept Numerions from stopping them. I grabbed the dagger from my boot and then I felt a hand on my side. I turned my head slightly to the left and realized it was Lewis warning me.

"It's not an average demon. You can't take him alone. That's a high demon. Perhaps the leader of the pack living just outside city lines." He whispered in my ear. I haven't been out in the field enough to understand high demons, but Lewis' parents explained to him how to kill one. I quietly and slowly stepped toward the weapons cabinet that rested beside the cave's entrance. I grabbed a Shadowsteel and tossed it to Lewis, then I obtained a Infamy for myself.

"Just in case my father is out there, I want you to stay in here." I whispered to him softly. He shook his head without hesitation.

"No, I won't let you get hurt. You can't kill a higher demon by yourself." He refused to stay behind which complicated things for myself. "Listen to me," I said a little bit louder. "I want you to stay here until I can confirm he's not out there. Then you can come out and help."

"That's really risky." He furrowed his eyebrows, worried. "Look, we're hidden. They can't find us unless they already know where the door is, which obviously they don't. Higher demons can kill with one blow, there from another dimension and that's why our demons use them as their kings and queens. Numerions in their dimension were a lot more powerful than us. Why would you risk your life?"

"Lew, it's okay. I can hold out for a couple minutes until I can confirm he's not out there." I whispered even softer. "I just want him gone. I can't keep looking over my shoulder every day." He nodded his head and put my hand to the curtain, readying myself. I looked over my shoulder at Lewis and smiled before stepping out into the darkness.

I jabbed my sword right into the higher demon's chest plate. It scrambled backwards, taken by surprise. I searched the tree lines and saw no evidence of my father here. I yanked my sword out of the higher demons chest and lifted my leg to kick it backwards, but the demon was smart. It caught my leg and threw me back against the tree. The blow took all of the air straight out of my body and I gasped for air.

Lewis lunged out of the cave and sliced almost all the way

through the demons stomach. Black blood lurched out and covered the mossy grass. Although, the wound didn't seem to bother the demon. He grabbed Lewis and threw him to the side, heading straight for me. Lewis got back up almost instantly, but the demon wasn't focused on him. Lewis struggled to his feet and lunged at the demon, knocking it to the ground. He was so angry that he shoved his fingers into the demons throat and wrapped them around whatever he could find, then ripping his hands out with the demon's vocal cords in his fist.

I watched the blood spew all over Lewis and run down the demons side onto the ground, creating a silhouette of blood around it. Lewis gasped for breath, he had taken a large blow and still managed to get up and defend me. I ran over to him as he moved away from the demons body, which was already starting to desiccate. I placed my hands on both sides of his face.

"Are you okay?" I breathed, looking at him intently. His eyes were wide, like he didn't expect himself to do that. He dropped to the ground and stared at his hand. I forgot that Lewis had never killed a demon before. When you kill a demon, whether it's a normal one or a higher one, you're filled with so much grief as if you lost a loved one. It's part of how they keep their species alive. Some Numerions are afraid to kill one because of the after effect.

"Hey, look at me." My tone was serious and I raised my eyebrows. He looked up at me with tear-filled eyes. I had never seen Lewis cry. "Remember, it was a demon that was trying to kill us. The way you're feeling is a last resort defense move for them." He slowly nodded and laid his head in my lap. I sighed and pushed the hair out of his face generously.

Lewis started to doze off so I decided to take him back into the cave. But before I could manage, I heard noise slightly to the left. I turned and was blinded by a bright light. I felt Lewis get pulled away from me. "Lewis!" I yelled, my voice echoing through the trees. I didn't hear a response. I tightened my grip around the handle of my Infamy, readying myself for anything.

The Infamy went flying out of my hand, I heard it clank against something in the distance. I felt a huge blow to my head and I went tumbling to the cold, damp earth.

"Athena!" An angry voice screamed, causing me to sit up too fast. I put my hand against my temple, only to quickly move it away from the throbbing pain. I was in a rusty, old room now. There was no sight of Lewis. I looked up and realized who had yelled at me. "Isiah." I glared at him.

"You don't call me Isiah." He quickly snapped. "I'm your *father*, not your friend." In his hand, he bared my Infamy. I glanced at it and he laughed. His laugh was sharp and full of rage. "Don't even think about it, little one. I'm older and much stronger." Really? We'll see about that, when I get the chance to slice your throat. I'll gladly watch you die, struggling for one more gasp of oxygen.

I thought about saying that out loud. But I figured that little bit of information is better left in my mind. I'll get my chance to see him bleed. He turned around, looking over his shoulder to see me. "I didn't want it to come to this, but you left me no choice. I just wanted you to join me in cleansing this earth from ungrateful beings." He felt that Numerions were ungrateful because we used every resource we had to help mankind.

"Ungrateful?" Now it was my turn to laugh. "You think we're ungrateful? Oh, that's rich. This is coming from the guy who brought demons here from another dimension. Weren't you grateful for the demons you had? And what about the children you left behind, were you ever grateful for us? Oh, and don't get me started on—"

"Silence." He said so loudly it came out as almost a hiss.

"Bring him." Isiah's voice was so deep, it sounded as if he was actually becoming Satan himself. Three large higher demons came through the door on the other side of the room. Lewis was in their arms, lumped over.

His chest was rising and falling to show he was still breathing. I felt my eyes stinging, tears threatening to fall. I shook it off and put on my warrior face. Mom had trained me for something like this. They threw him down on the floor as if he was nothing.

"Athena Grace, this is only a taste of what else is to come. Next will be Julia, Stella, and your mother." He said it as if none of these people meant anything to him. He has been around Lewis for years, even teased us about one day being partners, that a friendship like ours never stayed a friendship.

I gulped and Isiah must have noticed because he looked over his shoulder again, grinning. "Now." He said in a deep, broken voice. I tried to think quickly, looking around me for a weapon. I didn't see anything within my grasp, except for the Infamy in my father's hands.

"Screw it." I whispered. I stood up and as quickly as I could, I grabbed. I got it successfully and he swung at me. I rolled to the side, barely missing his blow.

"Now!" He screamed even louder. I may be fast, but there was no way I could take on three higher demons.

Lewis opened his eyes, they were dark blue and bloodshot. I started panicking. At this point, I don't think I was able to save him. On my left, three higher demons trapping Lewis. On my right, my father, ready to battle.

I looked back and forth between them, trying to listen to my head and not my heart. Lewis sat up, looking in my direction. He shook his head no, telling me I should take down my father before I lost the chance. Tears pulled at my eyes, this time I couldn't stop them. *Weak.* I heard a voice in my head mutter to me. I felt the drops run down my cheek, cluttering to the ground. It felt as if all time had frozen and I was standing there, everyone around me frozen. It was like the universe was giving me time to decide whether I wanted my best friend or the world.

Lewis wanted me to go after my father and take him down, save the world. But I knew in my heart, I wanted to save him more. The world could last one more minute, but he couldn't. I ran as fast as I could towards the higher demons, one turned to face me while the others put up their claws, ready to kill him. I slid under one of the demons, slicing it half from the bottom. Now I was in the center of the demons with Lewis. Lewis grabbed a dagger out of his boot, readying himself. But the demons backed up, my father stepping between them.

"That was quite a show, Athena. But your mother would be disappointed that you chose one over all." He simply stated. I didn't notice the dagger in his hand until it was too late. He forced it through Lewis' chest plate, sending him tumbling to the concrete floor. I cried out without realizing it. "You chose wrong, my child."

I screamed and drove my sword through him. He looked up at me, shocked. His eyes were wide as if he didn't think this would be the result of murdering my best friend. I yanked my sword back, driving it through him again and again. I finally dropped the sword to the ground, it clanging a couple times before settling. I pushed my father and he fell back into one of the higher demons, and then to the cold floor. The demons started to fall as well, because once their commander was dead, so were they.

There I was, the only one standing. I dropped to my knees beside Lewis, ignoring the throbbing pain shooting up my left leg. I pulled him into my lap and used my fingers to comb through his hair. He was still breathing, but barely. There wasn't a spell strong enough to heal him.

"It—It's okay." He tried to smile at me. "It's not your fault. D—Don't blame yourself f—for this. No mat—no matter what. Okay? This isn't because of you." I sniffed, trying to compose myself. "Save your strength, okay? Just don't speak."

"I—I love you." He said softly, fighting to stay. "I love y—you so much." He was choking on his words. Blood starting coming out of his mouth. "Say it, before it's too l—late." He muttered after spitting the blood out.

"I—I lo—love you." I was barely able to get the words out as more and more tears streamed down my face. He smiled widely, one last beautiful smile that was too angelic for this world. The color from his eyes looked as if they were turning grey, then he closed them. His head fell limp in my arms. I screamed, unable to hold it in any longer.

I heard footsteps coming from behind the closed door the demons had come through earlier. It came tumbling down. My mother was there, in the doorway. There was an army behind her, ready to fight. My face was already red and puffy from crying. She took in the scene before stepping into the room. She finally spotted me in the center of the room, the only one left breathing after the massacre that took place. It all happened so quickly that I wasn't entirely sure what happened. All I know is that it will be in the history books for all Numerions to read. By the end of my life, the story would be that I slayed all the demons on my own after they murdered the love of my life, then turned my sword against my father.

Whatever the story may turn out to be, we all know I didn't slay those demons. We also know that Lewis sacrificed his life for the children of this lifetime and the next. My father's reign was over.

TAKEN

By Tanner McFarland

ONE EARLY FRIDAY MORNING IN BIRMINGHAM, ALABAMA was like almost every morning: wake up, get something to eat, get dressed, and brush teeth. However, when I called for my dog Rocco, he wasn't anywhere to be found which was odd because he's the one that usually wakes me up. I immediately started thinking he was lost, hurt or worse, but then I remembered that I have four security cameras around my house. I went to my laptop and started to play each camera to see if anyone had come to my house or if I saw the dog leave. The first three cameras were clean, although when I tried to play camera four it had no footage, like someone had erased it all. I started to dread more and more, I went to my neighbors to see if they had seen anything.

"Ey J. R., have you seen Rocco? I couldn't find him this morning," I pleaded desperately.

"No, Blaze, but I'll keep my eyes peeled," he reassured me.

I went back inside my home to re-watch camera 1-3 while calling my wife but she didn't answer. "She had to have seen him before she left for work," I said to myself.

After looking through the cameras again, I still didn't find anything. I started to lose some hope. I went out back to see if one of the cords were cut and none of them were, so I was confused for a second when I realized someone had hacked into my camera and erased the footage while they were here...it was the camera that covered my backdoor so someone last night had to break-in—but nothing is missing except Rocco. I couldn't call the police because I am wanted by the Birmingham Police Department for burglary and fleeing on sight three years ago. Two hours later I called my wife and she finally called back, but it was from a different area code and she sounded scared.

"Hello," she said quietly.

"Babe, someone broke in our house last night and stole our dog," I said loudly.

"Help me, he got me," she said crying quietly.

"Who got you? Are you okay?"

She never answered, I repeated myself one more time, then the phone disconnected. I knew something very bad was going on, but I had no idea what it was. I didn't even know where to start because I can't go running to the police and most of my family hates me or is dead.

I got in my car and all my stuff was ripped out: like the radio, steering wheel cords, and even my seat covers were all gone. I knew this had to be the person who broke into my house and kidnapped my wife.

I'm going to find this psycho man and he's going to pay for everything he has done, I thought angrily. I have no idea who this "guy," could be. I just know that he wants something from me and he's a very skilled at what he does.

After searching all day I got a call later that night from an untraceable phone. I answered it and someone picked up. I heard something, but not talking, I listened closely and could hear someone crying. I thought it was my wife at first.

"Alicia," I said loudly. The cries turn into laughter, then I knew I messed up and it wasn't her: it was the Kidnapper. He was playing with me.

"What do you want?" I asked furiously.

"You have what's mine and I want it back," the guy said.

"I don't know what you're talking about, you psychopath."

"Do you wanna see your wife and dog again?" he taunted.

"Yes, and I will see them again, I promise you that."

"Give me what's mine and I'll try not to hurt your beautiful wife."

"No, please don't hurt her, she isn't a part of this, I beg you," I said desperately.

"If you really care about her then you'll pick the right choice."

"Man, I still have no idea what you want, just please let her go you can have me instead."

"THE MONEY! I want it back. You stole all of it from me," he snapped.

"Money? From that bank robbery 3 years ago?"

"Yes."

"Man I don't have the money anywhere. I buried that 2 years ago," I said.

"You're lying."

"No, I swear I can take you to them if they're still there," I said.

"Better idea. You go get them alone and if not your wife ain't making it to dinner."

Then he hung up without saying anything else. I knew I had to get to the Gulf Shores soon and get that briefcase of cash. My car was still broke so I called an Uber to take me there. I gotta make sure they are still alive before I trade them away. My wife doesn't even like it when I mention the heist, but now she's a part of it. I currently have $2,000,000 buried in the briefcase, but I'm not going to give him all of it or hopefully any of it. I have a few plans that could work, but I gotta meet with the dude first so I gotta make a spot where he wants to meet. But one problem, he calls me, I can't call him so I have to wait for the next time he calls. Around noonish I got an encrypted text with time and location, so now I gotta follow his orders if this is gonna work.

He wants to meet at Tallulah Falls, Georgia at 9 p.m., that's about a 5-hour ride from my house. There's no way I could ever get there in an Uber so I'm gonna have to get my getaway car in Mobile, Alabama and start heading that way.

Just got my other car, I've less than 6 hours to get to the location. I received another encrypted phone called again so I answered fast.

"Hello," I said.

"Did you get the money?"

"Of course, on my way there now, but let me speak to my wife to make sure y'all haven't done anything," I said.

"You're not the one making orders here, you need to shut up and bring me my money," Guy said angrily.

"How do I know she's okay?"

"Don't worry she's fine," the guy said seriously.

"What about my dog?" I asked confused.

"Well the dog is still healing, but he'll be fine, hopefully."

"WHAT DID YOU DO TO MY DOG, YOU PSYCHO?" I screamed.

"Your dog charged at me so I had to calm him down," the voice said coolly.

"I swear if you were to do anything to Rocco..."

"You have until 9 p.m.," he said right before hanging up.

I made one more call because I wasn't going to be able to do this alone, so I had the perfect person to help.

"Wassup bro," Trent said.

"Brother, I need your help I know I've done badly in the past, but I swear I haven't done anything in the past three years and out of nowhere some random dude breaks into my house steals my dog and kidnaps my wife before she made it work," I said.

"Woah, woah, woah, WHAT?"

"They took Alicia and Rocco, Trent, and he wants the money in the briefcase," I said.

"Briefcase? The one you stole?" Trent said.

"Yes, but there was over $2,000,000 in that briefcase so I only brought like a million. It was the only thing I could do," I said.

"So why do you need my help if you got what he wants?"

"Because I'm not going to give any of it to him and you're going to help me," I said.

"How could I help, I'm a retired Marine Sniper."

"Exactly, I need you to scope out the area with your Barrett M82," I said.

"My Barrett M82? This must not be good because that Sniper is for killing only, I don't scout with this type of Sniper you know this," Trent said.

"I do and that's why I knew who to call because you could never let me down bro," I said.

"This better be serious, where's the location?"

"It's actually right where you live in Georgia but he wants

me to meet him at the Tallulah George State Park at 9 p.m. tonight," I said.

"Okay I'll be there posted up ready for this guy," Trent said.

"Thanks, bro I knew I could count on you."

"Whatever, talk to you later brother."

Finally, after the five hour trip, I made it to Tallulah Falls, Georgia. After five minutes of driving around, I got an encrypted text with a location. He wanted me to meet him at Tallulah Gorge State Park but it's closed so he's asked me to trespass on state property. He really wanted me to get caught.

After I've made it to the State Park, I see a guy standing alone with his hood on. It definitely wasn't a worker so it had to be the guy. I get out of my car and start running to the dude, but not even a few seconds later he turns around and starts walking into the dark, I couldn't see where he was. Then I heard the guy yell, "STOP!"

"Who said that? Where are you? Where's my wife and dog?" I asked.

"Give me the money first," he demanded.

"I wanna make sure my wife is okay and my dog's still alive before I give you this money," I said.

A few moments later, a black van pulls up with bright head-lights blinding me where I can only see the figures of the people, but then I saw a dog's figure and knew it was my wife and dog, but someone has them tied up.

"There you go. Now where's that briefcase?" His voice was disturbing.

"Release them to me and I'll slide it on the ground," I said.

My brother knew right when I tossed over the briefcase, he's got to take the shot quick or this whole mission is a bust and my wife and I could both be killed.

As I tossed over the briefcase, I see him release my dog first and Rocco comes bolting towards me with excitement.

"Where's my wife?," I said confused.

"Where's the rest of the money?"

Then I knew the guy caught me and the only thing I could do is signal my brother to take it now, but he's got to watch it because my wife is right there next to the guy. As I gave the go-ahead signal, I was hoping he would hit the right person.

"Bang," the Barrett M82 fired quickly, hitting the guy in the back but he surprisingly got right back up. I tried to call my brother quick and to tell him he's got a bulletproof vest on, but not even a second later, another *bang* was heard.

The second shot hit the guy square in the head and saved my wife from being very injured. We then heard sirens coming from the distance so before we could even find the money, we all went back to Alabama. Next day, my brother came over to my house to make sure everything is okay.

"How are you doing?" Trent asked Alicia.

"I'm doing okay but still little shook up," Alicia replied.

"Let's stop talking about this incident and just go on with our lives," I said interrupting them.

"Well, you must want these back," Trent said while pulling something out of his backpack.

"THE BRIEFCASE!" I screamed in excitement.

"Here, you two need a vacation for real," Trent said, laughing.

"Not funny, Trent," Alicia replied.

"Well I'm going to go now, but I'll be in touch, brother, you know you can always call me," Trent said.

"Of course I do and later bro. Talk to you soon," I replied.

Six months later me and my wife and I were doing great. We have been in Jamaica for almost a month now and we really didn't want to go back to Alabama because we didn't want to be put through that stuff again. So we both decided to move to Jamaica and spend the rest of our lives here cherishing every moment. Of course my buddy Rocco is with us. He goes everywhere with me.

We heard a knock on our door. Alicia opened it and started crying, terror in her eyes.

"Who is it?" I hollered. I guess there is no running away from your past and the mistakes you've made...

CLOCKWORK

By Sophia Smith

FRANK WAS ALONE IN HIS DANK DIRTY CELL IN THOMASON'S Asylum. He picked at his worn down nails before standing up to pace. "Don't they know they are in danger of war?" he asked himself.

"You may plead and repeat yourself but you know as well as I do, Frank—they will only call you names. Your fate maybe the hangman's noose!" Seven echoed.

Frank continued to pace.

Seven roared in his head with anger, "Stop pacing. Why do you care if they believe you or not?! Let them rot!"

Frank tousled his hair, still ignoring the voice in his head. The voice still argued, "They deserve death. Be the savior and end them already! You will pay attention to me sooner or later. I was with you since you were a zit infested rat!" Frank shouted in anger, "Not like I had a choice in the matter! I didn't want to be burdened with a voice of pure evil!"

A guard of the asylum walked over to Frank's cell. "Shut up will ya loon!" he hissed.

Frank bit his lip and clenched his jaw. "I'm s-sorry good sir." He shuffled to his old cot and curled up.

Seven mocked him, "Good sir? Funny. I could sense you wanted to rip his gullet out."

Frank sighed and pulled the thin cover over his brunette faded colored hair. Frank was thrown in this asylum six years ago, he was only twenty. He kept up to date by drawing little lines on the walls, but then there were too many and he lost track. He watched the days change from outside his barred up window and kept the number in his head. Frank then pulled out a worn out old pencil and some not so fresh parchment.

December 3, 1938 Great Britain

This is the diary of Frank Alexander Hughes. I am currently in an asylum where I do not belong. All I did was warn people about an upcoming war, yet they throw me in this place. I will escape and when I do they will pay for having put me in this place. The only friend-like entity I know is a voice of mine named Seven. I cannot tell if it is a female or a male voice, but it tells me to do bad things to the people who put me in this place. You see, I am not like others. I can see into the future. I am not insane, I am a sorcerer. I hope can get out of here soon. - F.H

Frank became sleepy and paused in his writing. He did not feel comfortable sleeping in this dank cell with the eyes of the guards watching his every move. His chocolate eyes flicked to the window. He pulled the thin cover off of him and winced as his bare feet hit the stone cold floor. Frank often sat by the window looking out for hours on end. It was a sense of peace to stare out into oblivion and ignore the chaos around him.

Frank's meditation was soon ended by the clanking of keys at his cell door. He snapped out of his daydream and slowly turned. Most of the "visitors" had approached him with a club in hand ready to fight. He saw a friendly looking old man in a white long doctor's coat.

"Hello Mr. Frank. I am Dr. Thomason, I have heard a lot about you." He pulled up a seat and looked up at Frank eagerly. Frank didn't really believe it was good things that he had heard.

Frank scratched his head and titled it, "Hello, I am guessing you're the owner of this place?" Dr. Thomason nodded. "Sit my boy. I want to hear what you have to say about the future."

Frank sat down and crossed his skinny tan colored legs and played with a strand of his hair. He brushed it against his lips to calm himself, "Well, what makes me think you'll listen or believe me? I shouldn't be here."

Thomason sighed, "You were on the right track. We are close to coming to a World War with Germany. I would not be here if I didn't think what you had to say was important."

Frank crossed his arms and chewed on the ends of his hair with nervousness, "It's..a great loss to everyone."

Thomason leaned in, "But, what is the loss?"

Frank stood up and paced, "Young men, families, horses, most of everything will suffer. But, war will bring the U.S out of the depression because war brings work."

He looked out of the window as a starling perched on the side. "You will be discharged soon, provided a home, clothing and food, on one condition." Thomson said.

Frank turned, "I believe you want me to work for the war. But I know nothing of war tactics nor do I have any training."

Thomson nodded, "All we need from you is to tell us their next move and their plans. Can you do that?" he asked.

Frank's eyes darted around, "I believe so—" he was cut off.

The doctor looked stern and somewhat scared. He grabbed him by his jaw and spoke roughly. "You have to *know* so."

After what happened that evening, Frank's mind was too busy to eat his thin soup and stale bread. "That soup is poisoned. Don't eat it. They are trying to get to you." Seven whispered.

Frank sometimes thought, *"Am..I really crazy..? Is it just me..?"*

Seven started getting louder, making Frank's paranoia grow. *That bread is for chickens...it had bugs in it...bugs...bugs! They will lay eggs in your—.*

Frank groaned, "Shut up already, I'm not eating it anyway..." He shoved the watery soup back to the end of the cell, but his stomach grumbled in protest. *If they need me so bad..they should feed me better.* He thought. A guard opened Frank's cell and jerked up the small man by the arm.

"W-What are y-you doing? W-Where are you taking me?!" Frank kicked weakly and whimpered as the guard dragged him down the hall. Frank's mind raced, *Oh no...I'm- I'm going to be killed! What about my mission!? No!*

He was thrown into a room and the door slammed. Frank was too terrified to look up. He then felt confused, it didn't hurt when he hit the ground. There was a soft, velvet carpet under him. He glanced up and saw Dr. Thomason holding his hand out to Frank, with a kind smile. Frank slowly took his hand and stood up, "S-sir...did I do anything wrong?" his voice still shaken due to just being manhandled.

Thomson waved his hand at him like he was dismissing any bad thoughts, "No, No! What makes you think that..?"

Frank shifted his weight uneasily, "Well that guard, manhandled me like I was some sort of criminal."

The doctor dabbed his cigar butt into an ashtray, "Awh, don't mind that! They are trained to act like that." Thomson dismissed the previous conversation and took a sip of his whiskey. "I bet you're wondering why I summoned you here. I will tell you that after you have a nice bath and dinner." He made another shooing motion of his hand and the maids pushed Frank in the direction of the bathroom and shut the door behind him before he could respond.

Oh so now they are trying to drown you and poison you. How nice! Seven echoed and laughed.

Frank ignored his paranoia and started to disrobe. The mirror in front of him showed how malnourished he was. He gulped and stepped into the warm water and slowly sank down it with a sigh of relief. He learned from a very young age that he had to ignore his paranoia or it would consume him. He grabbed a cloth and lye soap and started to bathe. He felt so much better physically, and when he was finished he relaxed in the now lukewarm water. When he stood up he wrapped a soft red towel around himself and admired the fancy look of the bathroom. Compared to the showers he had to share, this was the life.

When he finished up in the bathroom the maids prepared a feast. There was turkey, hams, cakes, cookies, and everything fit for a king's stomach. Frank walked out slowly wearing clothes that were a little too big for him, and he sat down at the end of the long table. His eyes widened with surprise, and he started filling his plate when Thomson gave him the nod to eat. He filled his plate with everything he could possibly fit on it.

Dr. Thomson sat down with a groan of pain and let out a sigh, "You must be very hungry."

Frank nodded as he chewed on a baguette that he had dipped in gravy. He mixed his beans with his potatoes and ate them like someone would take them away.

Thomson laughed softly, "Eat all you want and let me know when you are finished. You're welcome to anything."

Frank took a sip of the beer from a goblet. He wasn't a fan of beer or alcohol. Frank ate most of the turkey, he grabbed both legs and ate both breasts. He soon became stuffed and leaned back.

Thomson let out a low mechanical laugh, "Now tell me what you see, what is going to happen?"

Seven blurted out, *FRANK! He isn't to be trusted with this valuable information! Do you WANT to get yourself killed?*

Frank saw a tall shadow figure move next to him. Was it Seven, protecting him..?

Frank ignored Seven and nodded in agreement. "I can, but can I trust you with it?" he asked.

Dr. Thomson's gazed turned to annoyance and soon softened, "Why of course! But I understand. This is information that is very important to you. Why don't you tell me a little about yourself?"

Frank was a bit nervous due to Seven's irritability. He took a breath and begin to tell his childhood story. "I was born in London on a rainy day around when the clock struck twelve. When I made my first gasp of air into this world, my father said time stopped for a solid minute. All the clocks had stopped working in that minute. My mother died soon after, but she was too ill to survive anyway."

Frank please. Shut your mouth. Now. Seven protested like an angry mother.

Dr. Thomson knew how to groom this naive young man until he got what he wanted out of him. He put his hand over his own heart and talked with empathy, "My dear boy, we do not have to discuss this. If it brings you sadness we mustn't talk about it."

Frank shook his head, "No, no, you're fine. I need to share this with someone other than myself and Seven."

Thomson raised an eyebrow, "Is this the voice you speak of? The devil on your shoulder?"

Seven gasped and clinched his shadowy fists and flew around in circles. *D-devil?! Why'd I outta—.*

Frank nodded slowly, "He...or in this case, it doesn't appreciate being called a devil."

Thomson chucked, "*It*, or I should say *Seven* isn't real! He is just a delusion of your illness that is all. Now, please continue Mr. Hughes."

Seven's eyes bulged out of pure anger. Frank shifted, and lowered his head at the insult. "My father and I worked on clocks for a living.. that is all."

Frank had taken Seven's advice for once in his life. "Your father died in the war didn't he?" Thomson sat back in his armchair.

Frank gave a small nod as he stared at the velvet rug. Frank heard the ticking he knew all too well. The ticking of time passing him by. His eyes shot to the old clock on the wall. Frank stood up and walked to it, "Cherrywood, roman numerals, and spade shaped hands...the time is off." Frank reached up to grab the clock. "I can fix it. An adjustment should do it some good."

Thomson nodded, "Why thank you. I've always wondered why I was late to meetings by a few minutes!" As soon as Frank touched it, it stopped dead.

Seven smirked and cackled and his reflection shone in the glass of the clock. *Tick, tock, tick, tock...boom.*

HOW STRANGE

By Harlie Webster

I FROWNED DOWN AT THE SIDEWALK AS I PULLED MY HOOD down to better hide my face from the cold wind. Nature's fall pageantry has no effect on me anymore. Looking behind me I see the good side of the town of Wolfwater where my waitress job at Tony's is placed a few miles down from the park. As I continued to its outskirts with its cracked sidewalk, it reminded me of an old junkie. The only color to be seen from the grimy street was the intricate graffiti and paraphernalia injections beside the sidewalks. From doorways of abandoned buildings came the dejected stares from the homeless and junkies alike, resting in their cardboard sleeping bags.

The stares were unnerving. My heart felt like it would jump out of my chest breaking my rib cage in the process. My senses were on high alert. Every color seemed to get brighter while every sound got louder. With my heart beating fiercely, I clenched my fists that were hidden in my hoody's pockets and brushed past them, my head hanging low. They began to pick at my clothing, the small and bony fingers latching onto me. I jerked away from them and walked a little faster. I could hear their taunting catcalls and cackling laughter from behind me, but I dare not turn around to face them.

"Aw, come on cutie. It was all for good sport!" one called out. I continued down the path and ignored the old hag. I hated walking this way, but it was a shortcut that would bring me to my destination faster. Walking down the streets and passing through alleyways I finally was making progress in leaving the outskirts of Wolfwater. As I strolled down the uneven terrain of the old dirt road, I couldn't help but look up at the clear night sky. The mix of cobalt blue and light Columbia blue combined together in a beautiful hue. Small white dots covered the sky as one dashed across it, and I quickly closed my eyes to make a wish. *Please, let tomorrow bring better days.*

After pausing to make my wish, I continued on the bumpy path to my 'home.' The wildflowers and overgrown grass danced when the wind passed. They brushed against my feet and legs as I stepped off the road and into the ditch, watching an old pick-up truck pass. The headlights illuminated the area around me, allowing me to see the fenced property across the road. Judging by the hay in the fields and the dark blue barn illuminated by a light pole beside it, I was by Mrs. Jay's farm. Mrs. Jay lives down the road from where I reside. She is a sweet old lady and acts like a mother figure to anyone she meets. I know this since she is a regular at the diner I work at. If I remember correctly she always orders a ham and cheese omelet with sausage on the side. Going farther down the road I could barely make out the dark watery hole in the ground. It was a dark blue that you could only find at night looking into a pond. The moon's reflection shined like the silvery sheet against the water's surface. The ripples darkened and lightened with every passing of the wind.

Beside the pond was the intimidating view of Western Meadow's Orphanage. The orphanage was an old Victorian home the size of any mansion. The orphanage generally had built-in terraces. It's an elegant, beautiful building with detailed designs and sharply pointed roofs. Don't let the beautiful exterior fool you. The orphanage was a place that had lost its splendor. What once was a lovely home, is now hell for the kids that reside in it.

I slowly walked up to the front doors. In no hurry to enter the building. The rotting wooden door creaked slowly open and echoing footsteps invaded the silence that hung like a thick blanket around the house. It's easy to say that old houses tend to creak, not in a creepy way, but more of in the, "I should probably get out of here before this thing collapses on me"| kind of a way.

This was a house that had you wondering if it was worth walking through the front door, more so living here. That said, I stepped through anyway, ignoring the stupid creaking. It wasn't collapsing any time soon, and, if it did, Who would care?

I walked up the old grand staircase placed directly in front of the doors. I stopped at the isolated room in the back of the hall. It was hidden behind the corner wall, so unless you lived in the orphanage you wouldn't know it was there. I opened the door and collapsed on my bed. I cuddled on my side facing my roommate, James.

James, in a word, is charming. His character is meticulous and mysterious. He seems to notice the minor things and plays them in his favor. He also has a propensity for lying, in order to avoid trouble and survive. And he likes to tease and nit-pick at people to get a reaction. But despite his negative qualities, he is a good and dear friend of mine. Loyalty is a good quality to possess, making others trust you.

James has been there for me at my weakest and was my first friend at the orphanage. He'd always stick up for me in front of others, even when he knew I was wrong. Then he'd let me know what he really thought when we were alone. I listened to him because he listened to me. Sometimes he could lose his temper, then it would be my turn with the wise advice. We were friends no matter what.

We are so close that the other kids used to taunt us by saying James was like a butler of sorts. And that he was raising a child so dependent on him. While I took that as an insult to my pride and my own abilities, James took it in stride. He even went as far as to call me, 'M'lady.' At first, I hated that name because I thought he was taunting me as well. But it kinda grew on me.

Later I had found that the kids were not meaning to hurt me and say I was useless. Instead, they were just teasing me about my height and my shyness. I've depended on James to speak and take control of social interactions. Since then I have been working on not being so dependent. Who would have thought such negative words could bring about a semi-positive outcome?

A smile found its way on my lips as I tried to silence a yawn escaping my mouth. I felt my eyes getting heavy and a small yawn left my mouth. I snuggled up in my covers and fell into a deep slumber.

There were flashing of images. Small sparks erupted from around the garden. From those sparks came a fire. The fire grew and grew until there was no possible way to escape. I started to freak out. He stood wide-eyed and trembled, as the fire got closer. My breathing was shallow as I gripped my arms with white knuckles. Then, a flashing of blue lights and the intoxicating darkness filled my lungs suffocating me. I reached out for help but nobody came. I prayed for a savior, but no one saved me. I shouted at the heavens 'have mercy on me,' I was given no such things.

"Koemi!" shouted a distant voice. "Wake up, it's just a dream," it spoke again. I felt something grasp my shoulder. I thrashed around, trying to escape the darkness. Soon the darkness faded and I was met with a blinding light. I closed my eyes tightly preparing for my judgment. "Koemi, you can open your eyes! I swear to you, that you are safe." The voice gently coaxed.

I slowly opened my eyes seeing a tall figure over me with his hand on my shoulders. The figure was one I was acquainted with, James. He had long elbow black hair that reached to the nape of his neck. Part of his hair was parted to the side showing his cobalt blue eyes. His face held a smile that was half genuine and half smirk. His pale skin was adorned with the usual dark marks from fights on his chiseled face. He had a black color liner thinly outlining his eyes, with dark circles and bruises in the shape of fingerprints on his neck. Oh, how I so wanted to examine his wounds, but I knew if I did he would shy away from me. The lower part of his face, on his split lower lip, was a lip piercing.

He wore dark clothing which consisted of a silky blood red button up shirt with the sleeves reaching his elbows, showing off his slightly pale arms. Over the top of that was a black vest with red lace designs. The pants he wore were tightly fitted and had a chain hooked from the pockets of his pants. It's amazing what you can find in a consignment shop. He stood back from me, standing his full six-foot height. He naturally held an aura of danger and mystery, which intimidated everyone. Everyone but me.

"It's time to get dressed M'lady. I know how much you love

Halloween! Do you need any assistance by chance?" His velvety voice asked with a smirk.

"I think I have the dressing part handled. I'll just need you to prepare and do my makeup James," I said, unaffected by his charm. I turned away from him pulling out my costume.

"As you wish M'lady." He placed a fist to his heart as if he was to pierce it, and bowed his head.

"James!" I called out teasingly, turning around facing him. "How many times have I told you to call me by my name and not 'M'Lady'?"

I placed my hands on my hips and gave a smile. Even though my lips held a smile my eyes held a warning glare.

He just chuckled at me and turned away to gather my makeup.

"Yes, how forgetful of me. Will you forgive this tainted soul, for the mistake I made?" He asked amused by this.

"For now. Now, please go away for I need to change," I commanded.

He nodded his head in understanding and turned away, applying some makeup to his neck as he stepped outside. I turned and admired my costume. I had to save up money to be able to afford the clothes for costumes, but it was worth it. My outfit was a bodice top that was strapless and similar to a corset, that being it had to be laced up in the back. The design was similar to a pretty night sky. On the bodice it had small shiny sequins place onto the black like the stars in the night sky. With it, I wore a pair of leggings similar color to the bodice. The shoes I wore were white slip on shoes. I put on my white collar and white fingerless gloves. All that was left was the cloak that I made out of an old curtain. Like the rest of my outfit, it was a dark black. It had a hood and fastens together at my neck with a string and it opens at the front to give my hands and arms free range to move. It was also short, it stopped at my hips so I can't trip over it. I turned to James.

"You can come in and get started now," I told him. This was our usual routine. James naturally wakes up early, and as he does so he prepares himself for the day as I sleep. Once he is done he wakes me up and I prepare myself for the day. Only on special occasions, he will gather the makeup I save over the years and do it for me since I become half-dead when I first wake up. Before our routine was like second nature, I had to teach James the art of makeup, and what he can and can't do. For example, don't use lipstick as eyeshadow. Looking back at the first time he did my makeup I can't help but think, 'Oh, boy what a disaster that was.'

He turned to hold the supplies needed for my appearance and motioned for me to set on my bed. Looking at the uncomfortable bed often made my back hurt. Seeing that we don't have many luxury items I've grown accustomed to being more grateful and humble. As they say, 'the things you take granted for is the thing many are praying for.'

We sleep in a small room, a vanity with a stool which was the only furniture we had besides our bed. I sat down as he pulled the stool in front of me. After a few minutes of him having his way with me, he lead me to the mirror to see his handy work. I opened my eyes and was impressed. Even though my makeup never changes I can't help but be astounded every time.

My eyelids were covered with burgundy and maroon bringing out the richness of my brown eyes without overpowering them. I had put on black liner myself since I flinch every time anyone besides myself puts it on me. On my lips was a rich red color outlined with red lip liner. The first time I wore red lipstick I was very uncertain about the colors until James said to me one day, "It gives a bold, dashing look to fair skin women with pinkish or rosy hues, like you."

"What do you think?" he asked me.

"Oh stop playing coy, you know I love it," I said giving a shadow of a smile.

Once we were on the stairs we saw all the kids waiting by the door. I looked him up and down once more before I was satisfied.

"Okay, let's get going. We need to head to the festival and then we will head to all the rich houses for the good candy!" I said trying to hype them up.

They cheered and lined up by the door, knowing that James and I would not take them out until they did so. Once everyone was lined up youngest to oldest (excluding me and James who held the babies) and their coats were fastened around them, we left the orphanage.

Halloween brought out so many of our inner monsters in a good way. Halloween people became whatever they dressed up as. Adults became zombies and murderers while the young children got superpowers. The lawns are now graveyards that inhabited plastic skeletons. Witches and Ghosts dangle from posts, while little kids walk up driveways to weirdly dressed creatures to fill up their buckets with their sweets. I let the kids roam around using the buddy system, while James and I followed behind. From past experiences, we have come to realize that it's best to let them lose and feel as if they have freedom than to chase them because they feel constricted. Nate gave out a shrill shriek of laughter as he saw a person dressed in a bunny costume. Neomi, on the other hand, was playing with James's long hair. James had a content smile on his face.

Time had passed, and the kid's excitement had simmered

down. With buckets full of precious candy, we regrouped and made our way out the towards 'home.'

The whole way 'home' was a giddy stroll. We were so high off happiness itself that we failed to realize the trouble that awaited us.

James and I had just put the kids to bed, and was headed to sleep when I heard, "Koemi, get your ass down here now!"

I was startled, and scrambled up from my bed, and ran out of the room. I made sure to shut the door as I made my way towards my caretaker. I looked around the corner and saw him packing up his briefcase, dashing from one side of the room to the other. His eyebrows were turned down as his eyes were squinted as he glared at wherever he looked at. His jaw was clenched and I could feel the rage radiating from him.

Suddenly, he slammed his tightened fist on the table yelling insults about me, causing me to make a small noise letting my presence to be known. He looked over in my direction with a harsh look. I flinched and held my arms close to me as my gazes shifted to the floor.

"Koemi, look at your father," he commanded. *Father huh? I wish I remembered what one of those were,* I thought. It was a sour thought, but it was true. I can't remember how it felt to have a real loving family. I couldn't remember the comforting smell of my dad's cologne or feeling the loving warmth of his arms as he hugged me. To be honest I missed that. It's funny, I miss my birth parents but I can't remember all the experiences I had with them. Other than the incident. A stinging pain on my cheek snapped me out of my thoughts. I cradled my cheek and looked up at my 'Father' with teary eyes.

"Now listen here, you dumb bitch. I'm going to work and will be running some errands. I need this house to be spotless and fix yourself up, we'll have a guest coming over tonight." He said invading my space, his spit flying at me. I could smell the alcohol and cigarettes on his breath. I covered my nose and turned away.

He grabbed my hair from the back of my head and forced my head to look at him. His eyes held rage and his face was redder than the devil himself.

"I told you to look at ME!" he roared gripping my hair harder.

I nodded my head and whimpered from the pain. My hands reached for his trying to tug them away from my aching scalp. I scratched at his hand until he threw me to the ground. I curled up on my side, preparing for the beating I was likely to receive.

Beep! Beep! I looked thru the gap between my arms and saw him about to hit me but stopped to turn off the alarm on his wristwatch. He said a few curses and grabbed his briefcase. He walked to the door but not before hollering that I was in need of another beating. Once the door slammed shut, I slowly got up off the ground. I sat on the floor with an undeniable sensation of self-pity and regret.

"You know you are the one that allows him to do it right? Abuse you I mean." James said nonchalantly. He was leaning against a wall, partly hidden by the stairs banister.

"At this point, I might as well deserve it." His usual calm expression was now one of disbelief and shock. He took big strides towards me. Once he was in arm's length of me he pulled me into a crushing hug. I hugged him badly with all I had and felt small tears fall from my eyes.

"Why? How could you say that?"" James asked concerned.

"I—I" I said in between tears. My voice sounded so helpless as sobs kept breaking my words.

"I know. We all have to go through shit. Sasha is having

more tantrums, Luke has become more of a masochist, and Sam is being distant," James ranted.

Knowing that the kids, my Family, are suffering because of me nearly killed me. My heart felt as if it was being crushed by a snake that had spikes instead of scales. My lungs struggle for breath against the prison bar-like ribs as I kept sobbing. James pulled me away, to set me on the bed with him beside me, and tried coaching me to breathe. He grabbed hold of my face and made me look at him. I looked into his sky-colored eyes and slowly felt calmer.

"That's it, breathe. I'm right here," James said soothingly.

Sooner than expected, I was fine again. I could breathe. I looked into James's eyes and saw the fear behind them. James had never seen me break down, usually, I was alone when I broke down. I began to notice that he was shaking and paler than normal. I reached out and cupped his cheek as I rubbed circles with my thumb.

In a small voice, I said, "T—Thanks, J—James."

That must have snapped him back to reality, as he trembled, "You're w-welcome."

Inhaling a shaky breath he said, "We have to do something. We have to go."

"What do you mean? How? We don't have any place to go!"

He stood up and started pacing back and forth clutching his head, pulling his black hair. His breathing was heavy and he kept clenching and unclenching his jaw. He looked scary. He was red in the face, like the color of an overripe tomato. Eyes squinting meanly, staring hard, fists clenched and slammed down onto the table nearby.

His voice held a hard edge when he spoke. His tantrums were immediate and violent. There was no winding up period, no warning. They were a full force from the very start like a bomb with no fuse, just an immediate explosion.

"James please calm down. I'm fine!" I shouted.

"Fine! How are you fine? How is any of this 'fine'?" he shouted getting close to my face. He was shaking in anger and I could feel it radiating off him. I backed up a bit and looked away from him. I could not bring myself to look him in the eye.

"See, there you go again. You always put everyone before yourself and all it does is hurt you. Don't spare my feelings." He accused.

"Well, I'm sorry that I care!" I said, anger fueling me.

"We will talk about this later. For now, I need to get the kids and hide them. Then we will kill that bastard!" James said with a frightening tone.

"James I know you're upset but we can't murder someone."

"So you are conspiring against me now are ya?" A voice roared.

Father was standing at the doorway, most likely coming back for something he had left. His face was the very definition of terror. My blood ran cold and I began to tremble. Father ran at us with his arm pulled back.

Without a moment's hesitation, James stepped in front of me and threw a punch at Father's face. I heard a snap when his fist made contact. Father fell to the ground, having his hands wrapped around his nose as blood poured from between his fingers.

Father stood in shock before entering a violent rage. James quickly dodged the fist coming in his direction, but not the kick aimed at his head. His head jerked violently to the side.

One would have thought he would have fallen, but the stubbornly stood his ground with his arms raised to protect him. Father came back with another punch, pawing at James' hand hoping for a clear shot. Only, James threw a quick jab before his fist made it any closer. He continued to circle him with continuous punches to hold him off.

"Keomi, take the kids and run! Run NOW!" James shouted.

It was from that one scene that put things in motion. I darted up the stairs and collected the kids, safely leading them out the back entrance of the orphanage. 'Finally, I'm free!'

I run, feet kissing the land. I relish the feeling of freedom. Breathing steady, heart strong this was freedom in its simplest forms. I had left the yard and traveled into the woods behind it. All the trees were tightly-knit, just one strand in a massive web of life. It was filled with rich, autumnal colors. The scent of earth and water drifted through the air. It was a picture of serenity. I found a familiar path and followed its trail leading the kids to safety. Once they were nicely hidden away, I ran back for James.

When I step foot on the property I felt uneasy. I felt a chill travel down my spine as goosebumps run up my arms. When I got closer to the manor I could hear stuff being thrown. I heard a pained scream from James. After that he was thrown through a window next to me. Glass twinkling in the dim light the moon gave. It danced in the air as it rained down.

He landed harshly on the ground with glass shards covering the ground around him. Without a second thought, I rushed to his aid. I ripped part of my shirt to help stop the bleeding coming from his head. I noticed glass was lodged into his once clear, pale skin. Even without any knowledge of medical aid, I could tell he would need stitches.

I focused on the bleeding since it was the only thing I knew how to do. Once I took care of the bleeding, I awkwardly carried him away from the house of horror to hide him.

When he was hidden I made it back and snuck my way in

the orphanage. I became worried about the others as I made my way down the halls. Every logical thought told me to run away from danger, but I couldn't. I had to end this once and for all.

The bright flames provided a spectacular light show as the old dark wood cracked and broke apart causing embers to fly, like fireflies lighting the dark abyss. Seeing the place that has caused me so much torment and anguish going up in flames, brought a smile to my face. Finally, we might have a chance, a chance to live freely. A hand rests on my shoulder by my companion. I leaned my head to the side and rested it on them.

"Go back to hell from which you came. Your hellish rule is now over, for the true queen has taken her throne," I heard James mumble.